The
Numbers
GET IN ORDER!

You can COUNT on them!

Toby D Morris

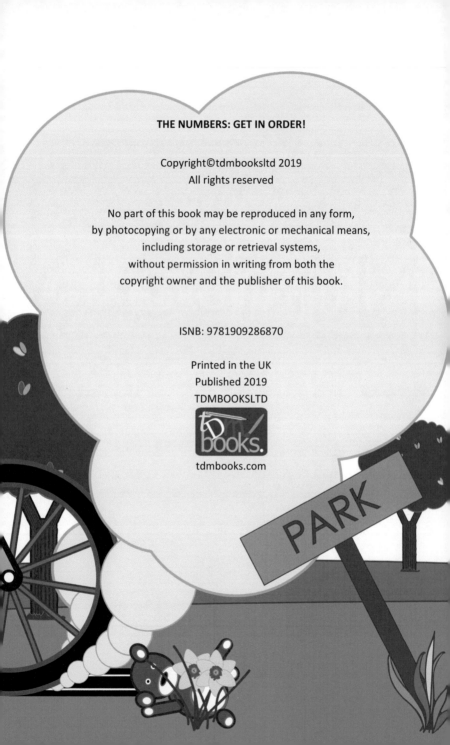

THE NUMBERS: GET IN ORDER!

ISNB: 9781909286870

Printed in the UK
Published 2019
TDMBOOKSLTD

tdmbooks.com

THE BIG WHITE HOUSE

Teddy Bear Factory

Phone Shop

Dance Club

Ice Lolly Shop

Airport

Bicycle Shop

COFFEE SHOP

Electrical Shop

Healthy Snack Shop

Bakery

FURNITURE STORE

Flower Shop

CouNt Modern

BANK

School

Science

UNDER EARTH

THIS BOOK BELONGS TO:

The Numbers

You can COUNT on them!

CHAPTER 0:

THOUGHTFUL

It may seem strange to us now, but there was a time when **The Numbers** *weren't* in **order**...

'Don't you stand **next to me**!' bellowed **66** before he inhaled, expanding his barrel-shaped chest; the buttons of his chef's apron were ready to **pop**.

'**I wouldn't want to,**' replied **67** sharply, turning up her music on her headphones and **drowning out** 66's moaning. They were both lining up, ready to be picked for 100's football team. 'You're *nothing* like me,' she added.

'And I wouldn't want to be seen next to you... *ever!'*

1

THE NUMBERS: GET IN ORDER!

It was a typical day, with the sun shining down on them, except for the odd white whispery cloud that drifted past. And, going by the usual commotion that could be heard all across town, **The Numbers** were behaving just as **disorderly** as they usually did.

On the edge of the park, **0** left her house and glanced over at 66 and 67, who were still **arguing**. She sighed, not at the chaos that **100**, their manager, had to deal with in getting the teams to be **in order**, but at her home, which was falling apart: the door handle was hanging by a **single screw**; the paint was **peeling off** the cracked walls; and the rickety picket fence behind her looked like a set of **very wonky teeth**. However, she was still chirpy and just as **thoughtful** as she ever was.

'Good morning, 66!' she said happily as she strolled in the direction of the teams. 'Thank you so much for baking this delightful birthday cake. I bought it earlier from your **lovely bakery shop**

and I can't wait to give it to 2.' She smiled, pointing to the pink cake that was poking out the top of the rucksack she had on her back. 'Oh, I had a **lovely chat** with your wife, **88**, as well...'

66 looked a little shocked. '**Oh... Err...** Did 88 possibly ask you where I was?' The colour was quickly draining from his cheeks. 'Sometimes, you see, I just need to escape from her... She keeps **telling me off** for not washing up, as well as for eating all her yummy cakes... Anyway,' he continued, taking a little glance over his shoulder, checking she wasn't sneaking up behind him, 'did you say you were going to *give* 2 the cake for *her* birthday?' he questioned, a little confused. 'Aren't birthday presents something we just give to ***ourselves***?'

67, who was still standing next to 66, nodded, this time in agreement.

'I've **never** given a birthday present to anyone... only to **myself**...' confessed 67.

'Well, I thought it would make a nice change this time,' expressed 0, thinking of the delightful cake.

CALENDAR			
2	2	2	2
2	2	2	2
2	2	2	2
2	2	2	2

'Although it would be nice to know **how old** 2 was…'

'Well, I've been 66 for as **long as I can remember**… As numbers, we've never been good at **counting in order**, or being counted on to **behave well**, as 88 keeps saying to me!' He giggled. 'However, I think it's a rather good idea to get presents. I'd *love* lots of cakes for *my* birthday…' he shared, rubbing his rather round stomach.

'I think 0's suggesting that we *give* presents and *not* just expect them, 66,' explained 67, taking a little look at one of 66's buttons, which was holding on for dear life.

'Oh, of course! That's exactly what I was thinking,' he responded, now turning red. **'Really!'** he expressed to

4

the other numbers, who had overheard the conversation and were now raising their eyebrows in disbelief. 'And I'm sure 88 would love the idea too, as well as us all being a little more **thoughtful** to one another... She's always saying I should be a little more thoughtful, for some reason...'

It was now the afternoon. 0, after feeling a little **stuffed** from eating so much birthday cake, had said goodbye to her kind friend, 2, and was currently trundling along Town Road on the bus. It was a busy bus route, and all available seats had been  taken by a group of **big numbers** who were going to **Phone Shop** a few stops down. A preview of a new phone was on show, and it was an opportunity **not to be missed.**

A few minutes later, the bus came to a halt outside Teddy Bear Factory (a large shop where you could build your own teddy bear). On a daily basis, many **overexcited** and **overzealous** numbers would leave the popular attraction screaming and shouting, desperate to go home and show off their unique bear to their friends. Today was no different.

'My bear is in-cred-i-ble!' shouted **11**, holding his bear in the air as if it was a world championship trophy.

'Yes, I agree,' responded **55**, appearing to be gracious before sharing her real thoughts. 'It does look incredible... *Incredibly bad!* Hee-hee!'

There was a degree of commotion as the numbers (and their bears) piled onto the bus. Amongst the mayhem was **81**, who looked a little sick. She hadn't been building bears; she was returning from the airport after working a **long shift** there and, on her way home, she had popped into Healthy Snack Shop next to Teddy Bear Factory in the hope that a cereal bar would **recharge her batteries.**

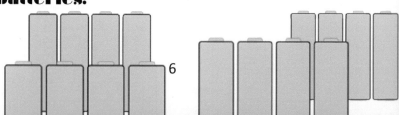

6

As she squeezed herself on the bus, 0 realised that, despite eating the bar, the best thing for 81 would be to **sit down** and catch up on some well-deserved **rest**.

'Hello, 81,' greeted 0 loudly, trying to raise her voice over the disorder. 'Would you like to have my seat?'

81 looked stunned before dragging herself over to where 0 was sitting. 'You're *offering* me a seat...?' 81 replied, still a little shocked at a number being so thoughtful. 0 simply nodded. **'Oh my!'** she replied again. 'Oh my! Oh my! Oh my! Yes, please!' she cried.

It was then that the other numbers on the bus turned around, noticing 0's rather strange behaviour.

'Oh,' began 55, who had just whacked 11 on the head with her bear, 'look! 0's being... err... what is that word?'

The other numbers scratched their heads as many lay outstretched on the seats, upside down and on top of one another, somewhat disorderly.

'I think it's called being **thoughtful**,' said 81, who now looked very relaxed. 'And wouldn't we all be in

better order if we were more like 0?' she shared, trying to give the rest of the numbers a hint of how to behave.

'**That's right!**' shouted 38, the driver, from the front of the bus. 'It's about time we had some order around here!'

To the delight of the big numbers, the bus was now at Phone Shop . 0 had hopped off the bus and was now easing her way along the pavement, **thoughtfully** moving to the side to allow the wave of numbers, who were desperately dashing towards Phone Shop, to pass.

As all the numbers rushed around her, 0 glanced up, feeling a **drop of rain** dance off the top of her head. The day had suddenly changed; the fluffy white clouds from earlier had now been chased away by what appeared to be a pack of **hungry grey wolves.**

The wind had begun to pick up and the sky was now totally black. Those with their new phones were

screaming in fear, scared that their precious item would soon be swimming in a **torrent of water.**

 'My new phone's going to die if it gets wet!' many numbers shouted as panic filled the air.

 'Out of my way!' screamed a handful of other numbers. 'My phone is worth more than *any* of you!'

 Numbers were soon knocking into others as they looked for a place to shelter, the shops already **filled to the brim** with numbers trying to get out of the rain. Some numbers fell on top of one another, and many even threw other numbers out of the surrounding shops so they could have their own space. Overall, they weren't very well behaved, to say the very least.

 0 reached into the side pocket of her rucksack and pulled out her umbrella. She was just in time too as the heavens opened a second later, water bouncing off her canopy and down onto the expanding **patchwork of puddles** lying on the pavement beneath.

'It's raining buckets!' shouted **10**, placing a magazine over his big head. '**Giant** buckets, too!'

0 turned to her left to see 10 frantically looking for shelter.

Without hesitating, 0 dashed towards him, holding out her umbrella. **'Here you go, 10,'** she smiled. 'Come and stand under this.'

Looking a little surprised, 10 ducked his head (and his broad shoulders) under the shelter. 'Thank you, 0. You've saved me!' he declared with a giggle, before removing the magazine from over his head. 'There aren't many **thoughtful** numbers out there; it's total disorder!' he added, noting the chaos around them.

'Well, let me get you to shelter,' 0 told him, 'but then I must help others before they also get soaked!'

'I've never met such a thoughtful number as you,' admitted 10, noting her kindness. 'I know it's not much but please, have this magazine. One good turn deserves another.' 10 passed her the magazine, which was filled with pictures of new homes for sale.

'Oh my!' she gasped, a little overwhelmed, as she quickly glanced at the lovely houses inside. 'I've always **dreamt** of living in a **lovely home** like these ones... But for now, I need to sort out this mess!'

The rain had passed, and the sun was gradually setting. 0 was at home, flicking through the still slightly damp pages of 10's magazine. As she did, she heard a **degree of commotion** outside. She assumed it was coming from her dream houses that were being built behind her. It was then that she heard a loud knock on her door.

11

After a few **moans and groans** (from the wet door), 0 managed to prize it open, revealing the face of her friend, 2.

'What a lovely surprise!' exclaimed 0 joyfully.

'Hello, 0,' replied 2. 'Come, I have a surprise for *you*.'

0 appeared a little shocked.

'Quickly!' 2 gestured with a slight giggle. 'But you must close your eyes!' 2 eagerly pulled her along as they made their way to the newly built houses sitting behind her old, run-down home.

What 0 didn't know was the **impact** she'd had on many of the numbers that day. They all thought it was time for a change – time to be a little more **orderly** and **thoughtful**, like she was.

'Right, keep your eyes closed,' commanded 2 as whispers were heard all around. 'OK, you can open them now!'

'Surprise!' It was the rest of **The Numbers**.

'Look!' giggled 2 as 0's eyes opened to see the flash of cameras and a large group of numbers from the park holding a banner with her name on it. They were standing in front of one of the houses.

It was a large, **white house**, perfectly proportioned, with a bell tower that extended out and up from the top of the grey tiled roof. The bell that hung within it was a stunning golden colour, and it now rang out, silencing the numbers who stood below.

'This house is for you, 0,' announced 2 with a smile. 'Your name has spread around the town for being such a great example to follow, and we wanted to say thank you.'

For a moment, 0 remained speechless as she gazed out at the numbers she had met on the bus and who she had helped in the street when it rained. **'I really don't know what to say,'** uttered 0, slightly dazed.

'Well!' boomed 10 as he moved through the large  crowd, holding a key. **'We hope you will say yes!'** 10 passed her the key to the house as 0 moved towards her new front door. 'You are the first number we have been able to **count on**.'

'I can't thank you all enough,' 0 responded gratefully, while unlocking the door. 'I'm just so glad that we're in **better order**. And it would be lovely if we could find **more numbers** to follow me. Perhaps we could all come here tomorrow to find one?' she suggested. 'But for now,' she continued, as she stepped inside her new home, 'please all join me for some tea.'

'And a lovely piece of cake!' shouted 66, holding a very large 'thank you' cake he, along with 88, had brought from *Bakery* .

As **The Numbers** cheered, 88 noticed that a subtle piece of the cake was missing. 'Anything you need to tell me, 66?' she asked, raising her eyebrows and pointing to the **hole in the cake** and then to the cake stains on his apron.

66 said nothing; he just tried his best to force the **cakey evidence** down his throat. However, as he swallowed hard, 88 had her answer as one of his buttons went **'pop'!**

'**Hmm!**' sighed 88. 'I hope that piece of cake gives you some energy… You're going to need it for all the washing up later.'

'**Gulp!**' was the last thing heard from 66… for a while.

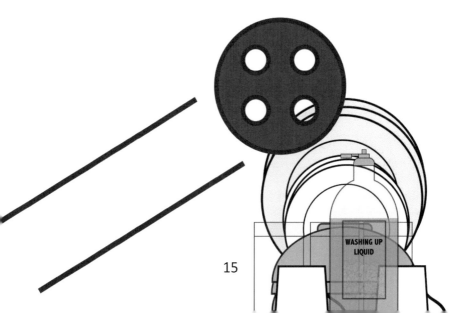

44

15

68

CHAPTER 1:

VOLUNTEER

'Phew!' panted 1 as he placed his hands on his hips. 'It always **feels great** when you exercise!' Keeping fit was always part of 1's daily routine, along with eating a healthy breakfast. As, yet again, he looked out at the lovely morning sunshine, he heard a *RAT-A-TAT-TAT* on the door. Not everyone's routine was quite as orderly as his.

'I feel so **unlucky**,' sighed **13**, the postal worker, as he passed 1 his letter. 'Every day is **hard work**. I never know what **order** we're supposed to be in. The only number I know who is in order is 0, at THE BIG WHITE HOUSE, but I have **no idea** what number should be the **first** after her!' 13 paused to

75

16

catch his breath. 'And another thing,' he continued, 'I've asked for some help, but **no one** wants to **volunteer**! I thought we were trying to be a bit more thoughtful!' he cried.

1 moved out of his house and patted 13 on the shoulder, glancing down at the large bag of letters he was carrying. 'Don't worry, **I'll volunteer** and give you a hand,' he offered. 13's mouth nearly **dropped to the floor**. 'Perhaps we can also help 0 before we see her later, by finding the first number after her **to count on**. That would also help us all...' he added cheerfully.

13 nodded enthusiastically.

After spending the morning searching and helping 13, all the letters had been delivered and 1 was now out in the town. He was on his way to *Bakery*, just for a little **tasty treat**.

'**Good morning, 88 and 66,** how are you both today?' asked 1 as he glanced immediately towards the **tasty treat** section.

88 and 66 were **scratching their heads**, looking **perplexed**.

'**Morning, 1,**' replied 88. 'Well, we're **in a muddle**, as usual... We have baked some great new cakes – especially birthday cakes – and we need to pop some into boxes ready to be delivered. But we're not sure **how many** cakes should be in each box. As usual, **we can't count**! To start with, we need to know the **number** that comes **after** 0!'

'I understand,' agreed 1, sympathetically, reflecting on his conversation with 13. 'We definitely need to be in better order, both with counting and... err... the way we behave... Perhaps a number will **volunteer** to help later?' 1 paused for thought. 'I tell you what, I'll volunteer and give you a hand counting these cakes, and I'll still try to find a number to be first.'

66 and 88 looked a bit **giddy,** slightly **overwhelmed** by the news that 1 had just volunteered to help. 66 soon **celebrated this news** by popping a **jam doughnut** into his mouth. He swallowed it, hard, and as he did his stomach expanded, forcing his apron to **stretch** beyond its limit and putting untold stress on his last remaining button.

Pop! It *catapulted* across the room, landing on top of a Victoria sponge cake that took pride of place in the shop window.

He didn't have to hear 88's reaction, as he could certainly see it; he turned slowly towards her to witness, beneath her chef's hat, a very **disapproving stare**.

So far, upon questioning, **no number** wanted to volunteer to be first after 0 unless they were **getting paid for it.** Feeling a little low, 1 made his way to the park. He hoped he would find a number there, as many numbers who played games at the park were always **desperate to be first.**

100 wiped his brow, took a sip of water, and sighed a long, weary sigh. 'Can't *any* of you line up in order *without* complaining?'

'There's no way I'm standing next to 12!' shouted 11 as he desperately shook his head.

'Hmm, really?' replied **12**, glancing down at 11's **basketball shoes,** which she thought looked old-fashioned and ridiculous. 'You know that none of your outfit matches, and your **shoes**... well, let's not even go there...'

'**Hey!**' shouted 11. 'That's just **rude**!'

100's head was now in his hands as 1 walked over.

'Hello, 100,' said 1 politely as 100 peered over the tops of his fingers. 'I'm looking for **a number to be first** to help us be in order. They'll be after 0.'

It took a while for 100 to stop **laughing**. 'Oh dear,' he began as he glanced at all the chaos around him. 'I have *many* numbers who want to be first. **First** at being the captain so they can boss everyone around; **first** at leaving to go home early to avoid helping me tidy away the equipment; and **first** to eat all the fresh oranges and drink all the water when we stop for a break. However, *none* are first at being a **role model**, which is what we all need.'

'This is harder than I thought,' confessed 1. 'We just need a number to volunteer.' 1 glanced across to the basketball court, which was just a **sea of numbers** piling and **crashing on top of one another.** There wasn't much chance of finding a number here.

It was the afternoon. 1 was sitting in C☕FFEE SH☕P, sipping his coffee and pondering. 'Where could I try next?' He sighed, feeling somewhat exhausted, before his **disheartened thoughts** were suddenly interrupted. The owner of the shop, **14**, wanted some **numbers to be first.**

'We're experimenting with a **new coffee**,' 14 began. 'It's called a ***Numberchino*** – absolutely scrummy!'

As she brought out a tray of cups filled with the delightful concoction, a horde of numbers *rushed* to be first. As you can imagine, the offer didn't go smoothly: they didn't form an orderly queue, and nor did they say please or thank you. In fact, all they did – as 1 watched the commotion unfold – was **dive into the cups**, knocking them **left**, right and **centre.** Soon, there was coffee and sticky caramel sauce **everywhere.**

'Hey!' shouted **44** as she went to grab one.

'I'm going to be first! Get your hands **off! Off!**

OFF!'

'If any number is going to be first then it's **me!'**
screamed **17**, barging his way through. 'Hands off *my*
coffee, **now!'**

'Oh dear,' thought 1 as he tried to remove some
of the coffee that had been splashed onto his top. 'It
doesn't seem that there's the right number to be first
anywhere!'

It was then that he suddenly saw **a reflection** in
the window. **'Hmm,'** he pondered, 'maybe there is…'

● had done a **fantastic job** of making
THE BIG WHITE HOUSE her home. **Daisies** and
lavender had been planted in the new flower beds that sat
underneath her front windows, and a stunning white

picket fence – matching the colour of her house – had been erected around the perimeter outside. It was, indeed, **very lovely**.

'**Good evening, everyone,**' addressed 0 to the numbers who were ready to discover the number after her. 'Before I begin, I again wanted to say a big **thank you** to all of you for being so thoughtful yesterday by offering me this wonderful house. I hope that, today, we can find a **role model** to come after me who we can count on to help us be in **better order**, as well as, obviously, helping us to count. So...' she continued with a smile, 'would any number like to **volunteer** to be **first**?'

'Does this mean we *don't* get paid for it?' whispered **55** to 60, who was standing next to her.

'So, do we have to be in order *all* of the time?' **99** questioned 100, who, like earlier, placed his head in his hands out of despair.

30, like many others, simply scratched her head. '**What are we going to get back in return?**' she asked.

0, overhearing some of the conversations, spoke. 'Well, a **volunteer** is someone who doesn't mind offering to help... for **nothing**,' she explained.

There was a little silence then, many of the numbers now understanding the real meaning of being a volunteer.

It was then, somewhat out of the blue, that a number arrived late to the meeting. **It was 1.**

'I'm sorry I'm late,' 1 panted, slightly out of breath, 'but **I've found a volunteer**!'

Many numbers questioned who it could be.

'Who is it?' asked 0, wondering herself.

'Well... it's **me**!' 1 replied happily.

There were gasps of astonishment that soon gave way to cheers. 'Hooray!' applauded 13, quickly followed by 100, 66, and 88. 'What a great role model you are!' Soon, other numbers followed in recognising his efforts.

'How incredible!' reacted 0, feeling a little overwhelmed. 'What a lovely surprise! Please,' she continued, 'come to the front, next to me.' 1 made his way through the crowd and stood next to her in front of the house. 'So, we now have the **first number** after me to count on,' 0 stated to the other numbers. 'I hope, by following his example, we can all be in better order...!'

With that the celebration began, and there was no shortage of numbers wanting to be first... **to eat cake** and **dance**, that is!

CHAPTER 2:

KIND

	Picnic List	
1.	Bag: *Check*	
○ 2.	Rug: *Check*	
3.	Cups and plates: *Check*	
4.	Cutlery: *Check*	
5.	Food and drink:	
○		

'... **Cutlery**: check. **Food and drink**: hmm...' 2 surveyed her kitchen. **'Food,'** she repeated as she scoured her cupboards. 'Ah,' she sighed. 'Not a pickle in sight! Oh, I do have some leftover **birthday cake**... although I need a lot more!'

2 left her house, along with the little cake she had left, and hopped on the bus to head into town. She needed to quickly grab some essential food and drink before heading to the **park** for her **belated** (late) **birthday picnic.**

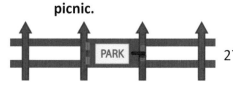

27

'Good morning, 14, I hope you're well!' said 2 kindly as she scanned the assortment of beverages resting on the counter. 'I'd like **one** water, **one** fresh orange juice, and of course, I'm dying to try your new **Numberchino**. But just a **small drizzle** of caramel sauce, please...'

The coffee was delicately *poured* into 2's cup along with a tiny drizzle of caramel sauce, as instructed. **There you go!'** announced 14, passing her the coffee. 'And here are your other drinks.'

'Wonderful, thank you!' 2 unzipped her bag and placed the drinks (with the exception of the Numberchino) into it. 'Also, 14, if you have time today, I'm going to have a **belated birthday picnic** in the park around 1 o'clock. It would be lovely if you could come,' she offered.

PARK

'Oh my,' replied 14, feeling little giddy. 'I've **never** been to a birthday party before – even a late one. Why, **thank you**!'

2 **mooched** westwards along Town Road, towards Healthy Snack Shop. As she did she noticed that many shops were celebrating 1 being first by having deals and advertisements in their windows.

*Be **first** to buy the new **Computer 1**!*

was stuck up in

*Get in order! Be the **first** in line to try the new **Bicycle 1**!*

was at

And, further up, past Healthy Snack Shop ,

was celebrating the new release of **Phone 1** – *the first phone with 'One-Button' technology!* (whatever that meant).

However, despite many numbers now being able to count to 1, and being in less of a muddle for that, they still needed to practise being, well... how shall I say it? A **bit more orderly** in the way they **behaved**. These things can take time to learn...

'Out of my way!' shouted **70** as he rushed by, skidding up on the pavement, showing off his **new Bicycle 1.**

'Hey! You're *not* being thoughtful!' screamed 21 in reply as she dashed to get out of his way. 'The pavement is *not* Town Road… **so get off it!'**

Suddenly, 70's back **tyre hit a nail** and punctured with a bang.

Flap! Flap! Flap!

it went before,

struggling to control it,

FLAP! FLAP! FLAP!

70 wobbled, Shook ,

and came to a halt, **millimetres** from a very sturdy-looking lamp post.

'I don't believe it!' he cried as he hopped off the bike and inspected the rear tyre. 'I need a **volunteer** to help me fix this!' he pleaded as he glanced around at the numbers who had gathered to see the spectacle.

21 smirked as she came over, holding a **puncture repair kit** in her hand. **'Oh dear,'** she remarked, trying to hold back

her amusement. 'I would *love* to volunteer and help you. However, I'm **not** doing it for free... I want a **reward:** an endless supply of Numberchinos!'

2 held the door open and waited for some others to leave before entering. Similar to **Teddy Bear Factory** next door, Healthy Snack Shop was teeming. Numbers were crowded around the counter as they waited to purchase a new healthy bar. *This is the 1 bar you need!* it advertised on the wrapper. 2 declined it; instead, she decided to get some fruit, with **apples** and **bananas**

being a must. Rice crackers were also a good idea for her belated birthday picnic, she thought.

'**Hello, 48,**' said 2 as she stood at the counter ready to pay. 'Just these items, please.'

'Morning, 2,' began 48 as 2 paid and popped the items into her bag. 'You've bought a lot of lovely things.'

'Well, I need them for my belated birthday picnic I'm having later,' 2 replied. 'Oh, by the way, **you're welcome to come** and join me over at the park. I'll be there around 1 o'clock. You can also invite your friends, too.'

48, similar to 14, felt a little unsteady on her feet. **'Wow, that's like something 0 would do... Yes** please!' she cried. 'I haven't been invited out for **a-g-e-s...** I must find something new to wear though; I'm starting to smell like **old bananas** working in here!'

Numbers were desperate to get their hands on the **One Box.** 66 and 88 were busy packing, filling boxes with one of each of their very best cakes: chocolate, raspberry, banana, strawberry, and a new **heart-shaped** cake – quite an amazing cake, it had to be said. Numbers drooled at the delight as they lined up in their usual disorderly way. 2, however, kindly waited for her turn.

'Good morning, 66 and 88, you have such great cakes for sale,' she remarked, glancing down at the One Box.

'Thank you, 2. To be honest, it's all thanks to 1. We're in better order now because of him, and of course to 0, who got us started,' 66 replied.

'So, what would you like?' 88 asked.

'Well, I'm having a belated birthday picnic today, and I need an assortment of **breads and rolls,** as well as a few **tasty treats** and cakes, for all my guests to enjoy.'

'Oh my, a belated birthday picnic sounds delightful!' expressed 88. 'I haven't been out for a while. You know what it's like: **work, work, work** and no **fun, fun, fun**.' She turned to 66, who was

sneakily putting a mini chocolate roll in his mouth, hoping she wouldn't notice. 'He's never taken me anywhere exciting... Hmm...'

'Well, you're both **welcome** to join me. In fact, the more the merrier. I'll be there from 1 o'clock in the park.'

Hearing his name, 66 turned around while frantically trying to erase the chocolate icing that had dropped onto his button-less apron.

"BIB I 'EAR MY 'AME?"
(Did I hear my name?)

he **muffled.** He had only swallowed half the roll. The other half (mostly sponge) was still trying to find its way from his mouth **down his throat.**

'Perhaps,' replied 88 with a giggle. 'Anyway, I would love to join you, 2. You really are **kind**. In fact, you remind me a little of 1. He is also kind and polite. Oh, did you know **he's moved next door to 0** in one of the new houses?'

2 shook her head. 'I didn't,' she replied, still blushing from 88's comment. 'It'll be lovely if they both could come, too.'

'I'll send them a text,' offered 66, now that his mouth was finally empty and he was fully part of the conversation. 'I can do it on my new Phone 1.'

'Hmm,' sighed 88 in a disapproving tone as she glanced at his new device, which he was proudly holding in the air. 'And *when* did you sneak out to buy that?' she asked.

'Err...'

The blanket was stretched out across the grass, under the shade of one of the large oak trees. The assortment of food and drink had been nicely arranged on it, ready for 2's friends to arrive.

'This is going to be fun,'

she giggled, taking a tiny nibble from her leftover birthday cake, followed by a sip of her delightful Numberchino. 'And very pleasant indeed,' she added before closing her eyes, taking a moment to relax.

It wasn't long, however, before the serenity was broken – a **swarm of numbers** had invaded the park.

Word had spread across town that 2 was having a belated birthday picnic, and so it was far more than those who had been invited that were now making their way to the park...

'I'm having that!' shouted 19 as he

wrestled 20 for a piece of her French bread as 2, now with her eyes fully open, looked on, somewhat in disbelief.

'I want crisps!' demanded 56, as he scoured through the packets of rice cakes. 'I can't eat this stuff... it tastes like **polystyrene**!'

Slightly panicking at all the numbers who had arrived (somewhat empty-handed), 2 was now desperately cutting up the food in order to share what she had. However, many numbers had simply helped themselves without asking, and without giving even a whisper of a thank you when they did.

'It looks like you need a volunteer to help you,' a voice spoke. 2 glanced up. It was 1, standing there with 0 and the other numbers she had invited earlier. 'We've brought you a few extra belated birthday treats for your picnic, and...' 1 looked around at all the disorder, and especially at a handful of numbers who were now **rolling around** in the last of the chocolate cake, 'we thought we'd lend you a hand too.'

2, somewhat relieved, thanked them. 'That's such a great help and so **kind** of you...'

COFFEE SHOP

38

'Kind?' questioned 0, with a light giggle, **'you're the kind one**!' 0 then paused for a moment, thinking. 'In fact,' she continued, as 43 and 16 wrestled over the last slice of Victoria sponge cake a few metres away, 'I think you'll make the perfect next **role model** to count on. I feel we still need help being in order...'

0 and 1 waited for the chaos to lessen as the other numbers, now somewhat stuffed and tired, lay out on the grass, ready to burst. 0 then spoke.

'As we are all here,' 0 began as several pairs of eyes, slightly shocked at seeing 0, turned to her, 'I think it's time we chose the next role model to help us get into a little more order. I suggest, by what I've seen, that **2** is a great number to follow.'

'What a great idea!' agreed 48 as she placed a box of fruit on the ground.

'I couldn't agree more!' added 14, looking very smart in her new dress. 'It was so kind of her to invite me,' she added.

THE NUMBERS: GET IN ORDER!

'Well then,' continued 0, cheerfully, 'I think we should all celebrate 2 being the next **number to count on**. And, we thank her for being the **kindest** number we know and for inviting us all to her wonderful belated birthday picnic!'

With that **The Numbers** cheered as cameras and phones pointed in the direction of 2.

'I think we should all have a selfie!' declared 66 as he pulled out his new phone from under his apron. 88, standing next to him, simply sighed.

Click! Click! went the camera on his phone.

2 blushed as 0, 1, and 2 stood in order, the other numbers also gathering around.

'There is **one thing** that has made this belated birthday in the park simply perfect,' expressed 2 as 66's eyes immediately turned toward the cakes.

'What's that?' they all asked, as music now began to play.

'It's sharing it with friends,' 2 replied with a smile. 'With lots and lots of friends.'

CHAPTER 3:

TEAM PLAYER

'Hey, it's my turn to make a tower!'

cried **64** as she deposited the giant pile of sand next to **25's** feet. 'You made the last one!'

'You just keep filling the bucket, 64,' replied 25 firmly as she began to mould the sand, hoping it would match her earlier masterpiece. 'I'm the **expert sculptor** around here, *not* you...'

Several numbers were getting ready, preparing their sandy sculptures ready for the sandcastle competition being held later at the beach (at 2pm). This year the castles were having *two* towers, celebrating 2 being the new role model to count on. However, counting to 2 brought its problems, as two towers meant double

41

the work. And double the effort meant that the numbers had to work in **teams** – a thing they found desperately hard to do.

RIGHT ROAD | BEACH LANE

3 slipped her feet into her flip-flops and grabbed her bag (and her phone, of course). The beach was a 30-minute trip by bus and she couldn't wait to see the spectacle on show. However, despite the convenience of the frequent buses that went there, 3 loved to walk, especially when it was such a glorious day.

——Vroom-vroom!

Beep-beep))!

Ring-ring!

The road was busy as others also made their way to see the event at the beach. Only a few had walked, like 3, and not all numbers took the bus.

Scooters,

bicycles,

delivery lorries,

mopeds and,

of course, the new **Car 2** – a sports car that had *twice* the power of Car 1 – were also modes of transport. However, there were only a few Car 2s on the road; they were far too expensive for the average number. Only the rich ones could afford such a luxury.

'Take a look at my *new* Car 2, all

of you *poor* numbers!' laughed **22** as she zoomed across the road, just missing 33 in his lorry. She had her roof down and her sunglasses on – clearly **showing off**. Suddenly, as she put her foot down hard on the accelerator and turned the wheel sharply, the car skidded out of control and spun around in a circle. **'Aargh!'**

she screamed as, along with the car, her head also began to swiftly rotate. This caused her expensive sunglasses to **fling off her head** like a frisbee before landing hard on the tarmac road. **'Oh my! My designer glasses are gone!'** she yelled.

Snap! Cr-u-n-ch!

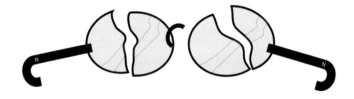

Hee-hee!' giggled 33 as one of his lorry's wheels rolled (somewhat deliberately) over her precious glasses. **'Hee-hee-hee!'** he giggled again. 22 was now crying. However, 33 just carried on laughing. He **wouldn't be shedding any tears** over them.

It was 1 o'clock and, after having a sip of water, 3 carried on towards the beach, passing rows of terraced houses as she went. Suddenly, she heard a **bang** followed by an unusual **flip-flap** sound. She looked down, wondering if it was her flip-flops. But the ring of a bicycle bell and **cries of frustration** made her look elsewhere.

'Not again!' cried 70.

3 turned around to see 70 and 21 (with her Numberchino in her hand) weaving and spiralling down the road, trying to control their new **Bicycle** 2 – a tandem – from crashing into a lamp post. Similar to yesterday, 70 had managed to get another puncture – his second run of bad luck.

'They need to clean these roads!' he exclaimed as he placed his head in his hands and sobbed. 'I just missed **hitting** some broken sunglasses in the road earlier, but I didn't see the **nail** lying there... **again!'**

As the bicycle rested on the ground, 21 – who had been sitting on the rear seat – simply sipped her coffee, leaving 70 to try and repair the puncture himself. While 21 remained chilled, 70 huffed and puffed.

45

'Come and relax next to me and take it easy for a bit, 70,' offered 21 as she closed her eyes, feeling the early afternoon sun warm her face. 'We still have plenty of time. Try not to get **too stressed**.'

By now, **smoke was coming out of 70's ears**. He was clearly annoyed and not at all impressed with 21's relaxed attitude. He wanted it mended now. Not tomorrow, or the day after, but now, right this minute, **straight away**!

'Hey!' he grunted. 'Let's go, **go**, **go!** If I was to wait for you all the time, nothing would ever get done. Move it! Move it! Move it!' he yelled.

'You're far too **bossy**, you know,' 21 replied as she began to rub a little suntan lotion into her cheeks. 'You're **not** in the **army** now.'

Just as 70 was about to **EXPLODE**, 3 came over with a smile. 3 loved nothing more than **working in a team**, and 70 and 21 clearly needed her guidance.

'Good afternoon,' she began politely. 'What a bit of bad luck that you've got a puncture.'

'My second bit of bad luck in as many days,' replied 70, shaking his head.

'Don't worry, I was nearby and I thought you both might need an extra pair of hands, instead of just your two. Perhaps we could **work in a team**?' she suggested, also glancing at 21. 'That way, you'll both be back on your bicycle in no time.'

The bicycle was upside down with its wheels facing the blue sky, and – with a bit of guidance and direction from 3 – 70 had removed the tyre, 3 had managed to fix it, and 21 was now putting the repaired tyre back on.

'There you go,' announced 3 as they flipped the bicycle back over. 'All done... and we did it as a **team**!'

'Oh, that's better, and thank you, 3,' said 21, again sipping her coffee. 'It actually felt good working in a team. You've done very well, 70, you really have. It's not often you listen to advice... especially mine.'

'Hmm,' sighed 70. 'Yes, it was nice to work as a team... for once. And thank you, 3, for your help – for helping us *both* learn how to be **team players**.' He raised his eyebrows as 21 closed her eyes again, feeling the sun on her face.

'Well, you're both welcome,' replied 3, feeling happy. 'I'll hopefully see you both soon at the beach.'

Beach Lane was busy. As well as seeing the sandcastle competition, many thought it would be nice to have a picnic on the beach, inspired by 2's belated birthday picnic-in-the-park yesterday. Many were carrying bags filled to the brim with tasty treats, especially treats that were from *Bakery* , including the **Two Box** – two of every cake you could dream of.

However, there was always the chance to get **extra treats on the way**.

23 and **93** were new to the area and it was their first time by the sea. They lived in similar houses a few streets away from THE BIG WHITE HOUSE on the west side of town. They were excited to see the **deep blue waves** and **the light-yellow sands** of the beach. Oh, and they were also looking forward to seeing **Ice Lolly Shop** . The problem was, they couldn't find it anywhere...

'I'm not listening! I'm not listening!' sung 23 as she stuck her fingers in her ears. 'Only *I* know the way!'

'Err... You've said that for the last **two hours** and we're still lost... You don't even know how to use your Map App on your new phone!' laughed 93 as he looked at his own, older phone. He pressed the 'One Button', then again, before giving up. Sighing, he gave his phone a really good shake. **'Hmm...'** he pondered. 'So much for one-button technology!'

It was clear that neither of them had a clue.

3 scrunched her hair back in a ponytail and wiped her brow. It was getting hotter and she was looking forward to a lovely ice lolly before the start of the competition. As she approached the series of small shops in search of her frozen treat, she overheard both numbers arguing. She thought she'd stop. Again, it seemed that this couple needed a **helping hand**.

'Good afternoon,' began 3 with a smile. 'It sounds like you're both trying to find the way to **Ice Lolly Shop**, like myself.'

'Hmm, we are,' replied 23. 'But I would have got there by now... if I was **on my own**.'

'Tell me about it,' sighed 93, trying to hide his confusion as he took another glance at his Phone 1. 'If I was on *my* own, I would be sucking on the **biggest ice lolly** right now!'

'Well, perhaps if we all worked together to find the shop, we could soon all be enjoying a lolly together,' suggested 3. 'It's definitely the day for one.'

'Or two,' 93 added with a little smile.

After a little guidance from 3, and all now understanding how to use the Map App on their phones, 3, 23, and 93 soon found the way to **Ice Lolly Shop** ... as a **team**.

'Oh, this was worth waiting for,' expressed 23 as she sucked on her lovely lolly. 'At least you know for next time how to press your '**One Button**' properly, 93 ...'

'I think you're right,' added 93 as his **eyes crossed**, feeling the effect of the two freezing ice lollies he had just popped into his mouth. 'And thanks to 3 for helping *you* be a team player rather than thinking that your idea of reading a map was right,' he sniggered, slightly sarcastically. 'Perhaps next time, we should *both* work better as a team.'

'Well, you've *both* been **great team players**,' commented 3, also trying to control her brain freeze. 'There's nothing better than teamwork... and a cold ice lolly,' she added, along with a **shiver**.

51

It was close to 2 o'clock. Crowds had gathered, music was **pumping**, and of course, the sea dazzled and sparkled like **diamonds** as it reflected the afternoon sun on its rippling waves.

0, 1, and 2 had come to inspect the sandcastles and judge the contest. Not only were they looking for *The Greatest Sandcastle*, but also for the team that worked well together. Unfortunately, numbers were struggling with the latter. Many **weren't listening** to each other, some **weren't sharing** (or caring) at all, while quite a few were being **bossy-boots**, shouting out orders to others. Oh, and there were quite a few **lazybones** too, who had decided not to contribute to their team but to sunbathe and eat ice lollies instead (although that does sound like fun!).

'Dig! Dig! Dig!' ordered **68**, as **83** lay stretched out on the sand with the empty bucket beside her.

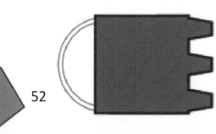

83 opened one of her eyes and tutted. **'Haven't you finished building it yet?'** she commented, slightly rudely. 'You're far too slow...'

Other numbers were equally demanding. **'What, 20?'** questioned 18, a little surprised. 'You think we should mix the sand **with** water? I've never tried that before and I'm not starting now!' 18 turned the bucket of sand upside down, watching as the sand just **trickled and fell away**.

'I told you!' shouted 20, angrily. 'Everyone knows it never sticks without water... You **should** have listened to me!'

As 3 continued to observe the **sandy creations** being made, she noticed that – despite many great individual efforts – numbers were struggling to work together. Again, under the blazing sun, she offered to lend a hand and guide them in the art of teamwork – much to their relief.

A little while later, the **overjoyed** numbers stood next to their masterpieces – sandcastles with two outstanding-looking towers, some with a moat, and many with two flags that fluttered like coloured wings as they tried to catch one of the judge's eyes. Not only did they build some magnificent examples; many had shown that they could indeed work together as a team after all. It was **quite a turnaround**.

'My, what wonderful sandcastles!' announced 0, cheerfully. 'They're possibly the best sandcastles I have ever seen!' The numbers who had gathered around, eager to find out who was the winner, applauded. 'After discussing with 1 and 2, we believe, as a team, that the **winner** of **The Greatest Sandcastle** is...' Numbers held their breath in anticipation. The tension could be cut with a knife (or a spade). **'... 64 and 25!'** she declared.

There was an enormous cheer as 64 and 25 went to claim their prize – **a giant sandcastle trophy.**

1ST PLACE

54

'Now, for the **prize of best team**,' continued 0 as the audience again drew silent. 'At first, I was unsure how well you were working in your teams. However, after a **certain number** came to help you, you all did a fantastic job being team players. So...' Again, all held their breath. '...the **best team** is... **ALL of you!**'

Screams of joy pierced the air.

'I don't believe it!' they all shouted, surprised.

'But the one number who we should really thank for making this possible – by inspiring us all to work well in a team – and who we think should be the next **number to count** on... is... **3**!' 0 voiced jubilantly.

There was delight in the air as **The Numbers** cheered.

'Oh goodness!' replied 3. 'I wasn't expecting that! But it would be a **real honour** to be in your **team of role models**,' she smiled.

'And to celebrate,' added 1 as he looked at 2 for support, 'we thought you might like to join us by having a lovely **ice lolly as a treat**.'

Other numbers also **froze** out of surprise, while others **shivered** at the thought, but one thing they all did as they stood under the glorious sun was to thank 3 for making it such a wonderful day, something they had all very much enjoyed... **as a team.**

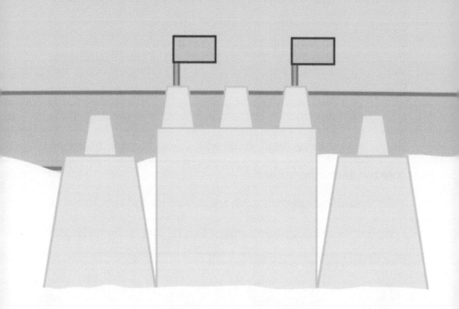

CHAPTER 4:

CARING

There were 3 ramps. The smallest was a **warm-up** ramp, and for those with the least experience of jumping on two wheels. The second was for riders who were a **little more confident**. The third jump (and one that stood nearly three times the height of the average number) was for the **DAREDEVILS** – the numbers who were the bravest (or just very energetic), who were now sitting on their bicycles in front of it, **ready to give it a go**.

Not one number had tried yet, but **35** had just put his hand up to volunteer. He was gripping his handlebars tightly, staring **intently** at the ramp. He was going to be the **first.**

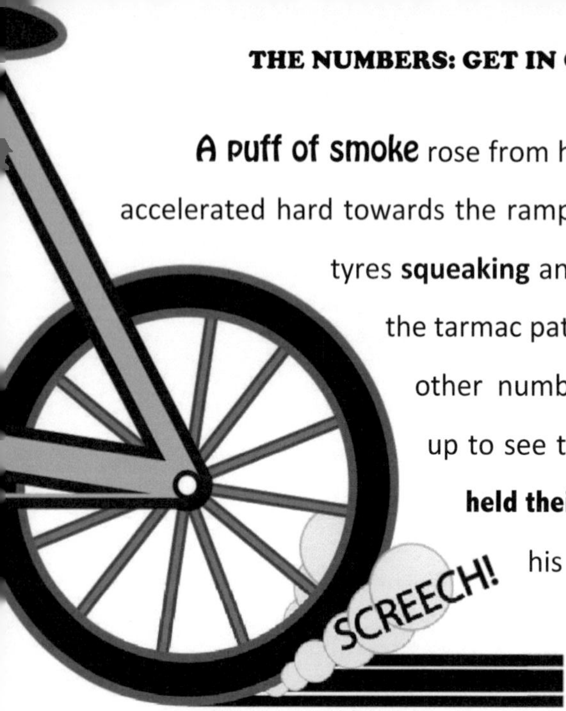

A puff of smoke rose from his back wheel as he accelerated hard towards the ramp, the rubber on his tyres **squeaking** and **squealing** against the tarmac path beneath him. The other numbers who had lined up to see the spectacle simply **held their breath** as 35 – and his bright blue helmet – went past them like a **rocket**.

SCREECH!

PUMPING his legs hard on the pedals, 35's front tyre touched the bottom of the ramp. Within a split second his back wheel also made contact, and he shot up and **ascended** the steep incline before...

TAKE-OFF!

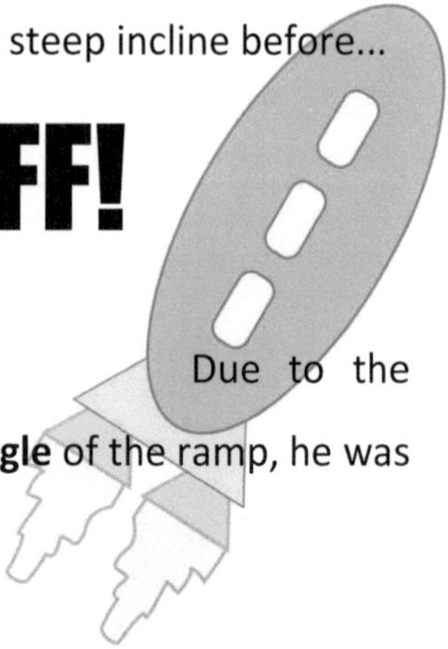

Due to the **speed** of his approach and the **angle** of the ramp, he was

58

launched high into the air, covering a **great distance** below. He turned, waving to the audience, as his bicycle – the new **Bicycle 3** – reached the highest point of its climb before starting its brisk descent towards the ground.

It was then that his confidence came undone.

His front wheel buckled on impact before he **tumbled** and **turned** as he was thrown over his handlebars and onto the ground with a **thump**. As he did he also knocked into 88 from

Bakery who was carrying the **Three Box** – a box now filled with three of the finest cakes money could buy, which was going to be offered to the crowd.

Gasps could be heard as 35 sat up, somewhat dazed, and shook his head.

You would expect the other numbers to rush over to help, concerned for his welfare and safety – and also for 88's, who was head down in a raspberry sponge cake. But their only real worry was for the cakes, which were scattered and crushed across the path. They did approach with speed, but purely to rescue what was left of the tasty treats from the box now lying in tatters.

35 slowly pushed himself to his feet as the other numbers dived into the spongy, **gooey mess**. It would have been nice if they were a bit more caring towards him, he thought. But then again, as he turned around, feeling something **warm and squidgy** on the back of his leg, he realised he had landed on the famous **Victoria sponge cake**. He smiled as he dipped his finger into the creamy filling. On second thoughts, he'd

prefer not to receive all the attention so soon, and be left alone for a little while longer, **enjoying his discomfort.**

4 had just been on the phone to 3,

seeing how she was after she'd been voted the next number to count on. She had just been her usual **caring** self. As 4 took another sip of her **Americounto** – one part strong coffee mixed with two parts hot water, **three parts** in total – she overheard other numbers in C☕FFEE SH☕P talking to each other about their day.

'You wouldn't believe the day I've had so far!' began **73** as she put down her coffee, ready to tell her friends about her misfortunes. She was feeling a little tearful. 'Well,' she began, wiping a tear away from her eye, 'it all started when the **washing machine** stopped working...'

'Oh my word, this is SO boring!' sighed **62** as she looked away and took another glance at her phone. 'I **can't listen to you** talking about your washing machine all day... Instead, I'm going to look at some numbers falling over and doing other silly things on the internet.'

'ZZZ!' snored **40** as she closed her eyes. 'Wake me up when you've both finished talking... Your talking just sends me straight to **sleep**...'

'To be honest,' interrupted 39 as 73 started to ball her eyes out, 'I'd **prefer** to talk about **myself**... Oh, have you seen my new **profile picture**?' she asked.

4 took another sip of her coffee. It was obvious that many numbers were still learning how to be kind and thoughtful. **'Little by little,'** 4 thought before getting up to see how 73 was. She now had her head in her hands and was in **floods of tears**.

'Good morning, 73,' began 4 as she brought up a seat and sat next to her. 'Would you like to have a coffee with me? I think it's always lovely to have a coffee and a chat.'

73 lifted her head, wiped away her tears, and smiled. 'That'll be lovely,' she replied. 'But excuse me if my clothes smell a little dirty... You see, my washing machine *still* hasn't been fixed...'

4 turned right and ambled along Town Road, heading for **FURNITURE STORE** a little further down, where they sold a variety of tables, bedroom furniture, and the new range of chairs. She wanted to buy a little **gift for 3** and thought a little **side table** would work well in 3's new home next to 2's house.

'Good morning, 17!' 4 said to the owner as she browsed the store. 'I'm looking for a side table. Preferably something a bit modern.' As she spoke, she realised that 17, who had a **saw** in one hand and a

chair leg in the other, looked a little down. **'Are you OK?'** she asked.

17 shook his head. He couldn't hide his sorrow. 'Well, not really,' he began as a tear fell from his cheek. 'I'm trying to make a **three-legged chair** – the first of its kind. But I can't make it **balance**...'

'Oh dear,' 4 sympathised as she again glanced at the saw and the wooden leg 17 was holding. 'I hope you don't mind me asking, but did you just **cut a leg off**?' she questioned.

'Well,' sniffled 17, 'as we know, a normal chair has **two** legs. So, to make a chair with **three** legs, I first nailed two chairs together. This meant I had a chair with... err... one too many legs. So, yes, I cut one of them off. However, I now have a three-legged chair.' 17 gave a little grin, pleased with his invention. His **smile soon disappeared,** though, as he recalled the reality of his achievement – a chair with a lack of support that would simply fall helplessly to the floor.

'**Hmm,**' pondered 4. 'I think what you need is a little help and support...'

'**I do!**' declared 17 sombrely. 'I do!'

After a little thought, and the all-important support from 4, it was decided that the leg should be stuck back on the chair.

Stick!

GLUE

'**Oh my!**' shouted 17 as the chair stood firmly. 'I'm not sure how many legs it now has, but it has **one more than three.** This must be the future of chairs!' he announced joyfully. Now with a big smile across his face, he thanked 4 for all her **help and support**.

After leaving FURNITURE STORE, 4 proceeded with a gentle walk up and down Town Road, glancing in the various shop windows before heading down towards the park. As she entered, she stopped to have a chat with 2, who was kindly planting flowers by the roots of the

large oak tree. They were in bunches of three and they looked very picturesque indeed.

Leaving 2 with her planting – and after agreeing to see her at THE BIG WHITE HOUSE later to help choose the next number to count on – 4 continued across the park towards the three ramps. There she saw **100**, who was standing next to his bicycle, **looking a little upset**.

'Don't let them see me!' whispered 100 as three DAREDEVIL riders came whizzing past at speed. **'They mustn't know!'**

4 looked a little baffled as she turned briefly away from 100. Her confusion quickly turned to sadness, however, as one of the DAREDEVILS came off the path and cut across the grass – and straight over 2's newly planted flowers, crushing them into the ground with his back tyre. 4 sighed before looking back. 'Sorry, 100. Why are you upset, and why don't you want to be seen?' she asked with concern.

'Well,' he began, still a little nervous, 'lots of numbers have managed to jump ramp one, and some have even jumped ramp two, and then you have the fearless (or just very energetic) **DAREDEVILS** who have jumped ramp three!' 100 lowered his head, feeling somewhat ashamed.

'What's the problem?' 4 asked. 'You can tell me, **I won't laugh**.'

'Well, **I can't even ride a bicycle** let alone jump over one of these ramps, and I'm the manager of the teams!' he disclosed. 'I should be good at **everything**!'

'Oh dear,' consoled 4 as she came closer. 'You can't be good at *everything*. But don't worry, I'll help you; I'll give you the support you need in order for you to ride your bicycle.'

A while later – after a little assistance, and some **encouragement** from 4 – 100 was now able to ride his bicycle.

'YOU'VE BEEN AMAZING!' 100 thanked her ecstatically. 'I can't believe I'm actually riding a bicycle. You've been so **caring** towards me. Thank you for your support and for giving me the confidence to keep trying.

Thank you again!' With a little skid, 100 then zoomed off into the distance.

━━━━━━━━━━━━━━━━━━━━━━━━━━

━━━━━━━━━━━━━━━━━━━━━━━━━━

The sun was setting behind THE BIG WHITE HOUSE as 4 took her seat — along with the other numbers — on one of the three-legged (plus one) chairs that had been set out in orderly lines in front. There was also a bit of banging and crashing as a new ramp (called *The Leap of Faith Jump)* was being erected, ready for the DAREDEVILS later.

Soon 0 opened her front door and exited along with 1, 2, and 3.

'Good evening,' began 0 as she scanned the crowd for appropriate candidates for the next role model. 'I've had a lovely day today with 1, 2, and 3. I must say, it's so nice to have such **caring friends** to chat and share our thoughts with, especially now we're getting busier. So, we thought it would be lovely to have a **caring role model** to count on next,' she added, a little excited. 0 paused as many numbers began to whisper amongst themselves. As they did, another number, who had been helped by a caring number earlier, **sat on his bike** out by *The Leap of Faith Jump* – a **giant** amongst jumps – that had just been finished.

Burnt rubber filled the air as **100**, now at full ferocity, roared towards the ramp. DAREDEVILS and other numbers looked on in amazement as 100 hit the edge of the giant slope.

Boom-boom! Up and up he went, far higher than any number had gone before him. And then… silence…

He was in the air, and as he flew across the sky he held a flag out behind him. On it were written the words, "THANK YOU 4!".

100 seemed to be suspended above the ground forever, before… **Bang! CRASH! Boing!** He hit the earth with a **thump**. Unfortunately, he also knocked into 66 from *Bakery* , who was carrying a **box of cakes** in celebration of the next role model. Similar

to what had happened during 35's attempt earlier in the day, there was soon a big **gooey mess.**

Numbers rose to their feet and many, including 4, rushed towards the incident. **'Oh my!'** she gasped as 66 and 100 pulled themselves out of the remains of a luxury chocolate cake.

For a moment, 100 remained silent. He simply **dipped his finger** into the **chocolate fondant** as other numbers crowded around him. **'Hmm, not bad!'** He then turned to 4. 'I just wanted to say thank you, 4, for being so caring towards me earlier...'

'And us, 4!' other numbers added, who she had also helped earlier.

4 stood there, slightly embarrassed. 'You're welcome, and what a way to do it!' she replied to 100. 'And thank you to you all,' she added, a little shyly.

'Well,' continued 0, looking at all the numbers 4 had been caring to, including 100, who was now licking his lips, 'it looks like we have our **new role model – 4**!' she exclaimed.

There were cheers as 1, 2, and 3 also came to congratulate her before an explosion of camera flashes went off.

Again, 4 looked a little embarrassed under the dazzling lights as **The Numbers** continued to cheer. 'I really don't know what to say,' she admitted, before her eyes turned back towards the **chocolatey mess** under 100 and 66's feet, 'except… I wouldn't mind if could try some of that cake. It does look **rather nice**…'

'**'OO 'AN 'AY 'AT 'ABANE** (you can say that again),' added 66, who already had half of it in his mouth.

With that, they all had a piece. **Sharing is caring**, after all.

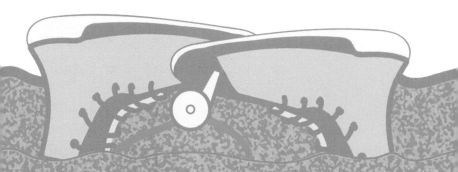

CHAPTER 5:

CALM

It had been a busy week for all. 0 had moved into THE BIG WHITE 🏠OUSE ; there had been a belated **birthday picnic** in the park; a **sandcastle competition** at the beach; and of course, there had been 100's daring attempt at *The Leap of Faith Jump*, which had ended in a large gooey mess.

Thankfully, with the addition of 4, **The Numbers** could now **count in order** to 4 (which made 13's job a little easier). Also, with her help and guidance, they were also slightly **better behaved**.

However, as you can imagine, with all the new things that were being made now that they could count to greater numbers, some were finding it hard to keep **calm and in order...**

"YOU'RE OUT, 44!" shouted **86** joyfully.

'What? Are you **kidding**? The ball was **in**!' screamed 44 as she stamped her foot on the ground in frustration. 'I'm not out! **It's not fair**!'

'You *are* out!' declared the rest of the numbers who were playing champ (or **four square** as it was also called, named after 4) with her in the park.

'You *never* get out, 44,' added 90, who was standing next in line, waiting to play. '*You're* not being fair by staying in. We want a go!'

'I *am* fair, 90!' she replied, feeling tearful. 'Actually, none of you are fair because you all teamed up to get me out! Well, I'm leaving then... *And* I'm going to tell 3 that you've all been working *badly* in a team! **Boo-hoo!**'

With that, she stormed off in a **tearful tantrum**.

5 walked across the park. He paused as 44 strode out across the grass in front of him and then slumped down, head in her hands, under the large oak tree.

Sounds of applause could be heard as 5 continued on in the direction of the champ square. 100 had arrived and several other numbers had also gathered around him, celebrating his **extraordinary achievement** yesterday.

'**Thank you, thank you,**' replied 100 to those who had applauded, lifting his hand as a sign of acknowledgement. 'Honestly, I can't take all the credit for my incredible **feat of bravery**; I must **thank 4**, who gave me the support I needed when I couldn't even...' 100 paused, reflecting on the time when he couldn't even **ride his bicycle**. He decided, mostly out of pride, not to mention that time. 'Anyway, thank you again. Now, **let's play a new game**. How about softball?'

Boo-hoo!' cried **86**.

'**No!**' shouted **18** as she frantically shook her head.

'Yes, please!' screamed **54** as she jumped up and down on the spot.

'I *hate* **softball!**' yelled **90** as he fell to floor, kicking his feet and thumping his fists on the ground.

'Ooh,' thought 5 to himself as he came over. 'I'd quite like a game of softball.'

After a while of discussion and tears, they eventually settled on a game of softball. 100 decided that it was best to have **two teams** of **four** numbers. He had **just chosen** the green team and was **now ready** to choose the pink.

'**90, 31, 97, and 45,**' he began as the rest of the numbers eagerly waited, 'you can all line up. You're going to be on the **pink team**,' he instructed, pointing to the pink bibs that were in a pile on the floor.

'**I hate wearing pink!**' announced 90, defiantly crossing his arms in protest.

'**And you look so silly in it!**' laughed 45.

'**Me too!**' added 31 as he reluctantly put on his bib. 'I also hate wearing pink!'

100 sighed before continuing. 'And 54, 18, 86, and 5… just to say that you're *not* picked this time, and you will have to wait for the next game.'

Without thinking, 86 immediately went over to the pile of bibs. He clearly **hadn't listened** to 100's instructions.

'**Hey, 86!**' shouted 90 as he shook his head. '100 said you're *not* picked for the team.'

86 froze as the realisation set in. He then turned around and sobbed. The sobbing turned into crying and the crying turned into **hysteria**.

86 wasn't the only one displaying their disappointment. 18 was also **balling her eyes out** while 54, like 44 earlier, had simply stormed off in a huff, a tantrum, an uncontrolled **outburst of anger.**

'**I'm feeling a little upset, too,**' thought 5 to himself, as he tried to **balance his emotions**. 'I would have loved to have played in the team...' 5 took a deep breath, exhaled slowly, and **calmed his thoughts**. 'Perhaps I can play later. I don't want to end up feeling too upset and ill over not being picked,' he reminded himself.

After the softball game had been played, another set of teams were ready to be picked for the next game.

'**Right,**' began 100 as he looked at the numbers who were still waiting. 'For those who **haven't** played yet... please get yourself either a green or pink bib. **You can decide** which team you're in,' he added, with the addition of a sigh. 'I really don't get paid enough to make all the decisions,' he thought.

There was a scramble for the bibs as many numbers screamed and shouted in delight at the thought of playing. 86, now with a green bib, threw it over his head and began zooming around the park, **partially blindfolded,** unable to control his delight. It wasn't until he **BUMPED** into the large oak tree that he came to an abrupt stop – much to the delight of 44, who thought he deserved it for getting her out of champ.

'Oh my!' gasped 5, feeling slightly overwhelmed. 'I really, *really* can't wait to play!' 5 had begun to feel a little giddy with all the excitement, so he decided to take a very deep breath. '*Aaagggghhhhh!*'

he exhaled. '**Let's breathe!** I'm excited about playing, but it's better if I can **stay calm**. That way I can concentrate and play a better game!'

100 turned to 5 and smiled, noticing 5's **self-control**. He wished that every number was a little more like him.

Teddy Bear Factory was heaving,

crammed, at breaking point, **full to the brim** with numbers. There was huge excitement in the air as numbers now had a *fourth* choice of colour for their bears. Not only was there red, blue, and pink, but there was **yellow** now too. And, of course, you could have as many combinations as you liked: a blue body, red head, pink legs, and yellow arms; or a pink body, blue head, yellow legs, and red arms, to name a few.

Eagerly, 5 stepped off the bus on Town Road and went into the shop. He was greeted by some (very) happy numbers.

'Take a look at my bear!' yelled

61, as he threw his bear in the air. 'It's got to be the best in the **world**!'

'You wish,' giggled 16. 'No one likes a redhead. Yellow is the fashionable colour now...'

79

'Yours is the best in the world?' queried 27, somewhat sarcastically. 'Well, let me tell you *all* something... **mine's the best in the universe!'**

'Not with **four heads** it isn't,' both 61 and 16 sniggered.

There were a number of show-offs, all desperate and eager to display their bear to the world – or the universe, for that matter. 5 hoped he could do the same as he looked around the shop and at the giant tubs of colourful bear body parts. He began to **shake** a little out of excitement. However, trying to **steady himself,** 5 took a breath just like before, managing to control his overexcitement. '**KEEP CALM,**' he thought.

A yellow head was stuck on a yellow body, and yellow arms and legs soon joined them to form what had never been seen before – a totally yellow bear. Numbers turned as **5 looked at his creation**. It was incredible and, much like the design of the four-legged chair, something that deserved a place in **CouNt Modern** (a state-of-the-art design centre).

Click! Phone 4s, with their **quad-lens** cameras, were frantically pulled from pockets. Suddenly, 5 was caught in an explosion of flashing lights as pictures were taken of him holding his masterpiece.

'Oh my,' he said to himself, grasping his bear tightly. 'I'm trying to keep **calm and balanced**, but this is totally unexpected. I'm trying my best not to be a show-off.'

However, not all numbers were as eager to celebrate 5's creation.

'I want a bear like that!' cried **27** as she looked down at her four-headed bear.

'I'm telling you,' began 61, a little frustrated and angry that 5 had got all the publicity, 'my bear is the one you should be photographing. **My bear is all red!** And...'

'And,' interrupted 16, 'that's **yesterday's fashion.'**

5 was in C☕FFEE SH☕P, along with his bear, lounging back in one of the comfy armchairs and drinking a herbal tea. However, as he glanced around, he noticed that many numbers were now running around after drinking the somewhat sugary **Numbrero** – a drink made with **caramel** *and* **chocolate**. It had quite an effect on the numbers who drank it.

Screams and shouts filled C☕FFEE SH☕P as the caramel-chocolate concoction ran through the little numbers' veins. However, those who had drunk it earlier were now **crashed out on the floor**, fast asleep, as the sugary effect had worn off.

5 again sipped his tea, remaining calm – much to the relief of 14, as they both watched the spectacle. 5 preferred to feel **more relaxed**, especially since they all had to visit 0 and the other role models soon at

THE BIG WHITE HOUSE.

0 stood outside the house along with 1, 2, 3, and 4. Anticipation was high yet again, with many numbers feeling rather excited. Although, a handful were still feeling the end effects of the Numbrero and were lifelessly **slumped in their chairs**.

'Good evening, everyone,' greeted 0. 'I can't believe it's just been a day since 4 was chosen to join our team of role models. I'm sure you're all starting to feel the benefit of being in **better order**. I can also imagine how the constant improvements and extra things to see and do can make us feel very excited. However, there's always a balance between being excited and... well...

being so 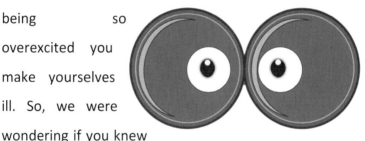 overexcited you make yourselves ill. So, we were wondering if you knew of any number who could help us be a little **calmer** at times?'

I am definitely the next role model,' boasted **49** as she strutted up and down like a **peacock**. 'I'm a winner. I'm clearly the best.'

'**Show-off!**' shouted **96** before lowering her head and crying. 'I never, ever, ever get chosen!' she balled.

'**I'm so excited to find out!** And I mean super, *super* excited!' screamed **63** as he jumped up and down before running around and around. He came to a sudden stop when he bumped into 100 who simply stood there, arms folded, shaking his head. It was clear to him – as well as a few others who had witnessed his behaviour earlier – that there was only **one number for the job.**

Those that knew shouted out the answer. **'5!'** they all cried.

'Well,' began 0 again, 'I'm glad we have now found a number. And I can see by **5's behaviour** that he looks to be the exact number we need – he has great **self-control**.'

'**Oh my!**' quivered 5, slightly shocked at the outcome. 'This is a *total* surprise.'

With the help of the other role models, 5 was assisted to the front as 0 quickly popped into her house.

5 continued breathing deeply until 0 emerged again with a rather delicious-looking cake.

'Here you go, 5,' offered 0, passing him the cake. 'This is for you!'

'Amazing!' gasped 5, feeling somewhat dizzy as the other numbers in front of the house **puffed** and **panted**, straining and waiting as calmly as they could for a piece. 'I would love a slice,' he expressed as his lips tingled, and his body began to gently shake. **'Actually…'** he added as his eyes began to cross, 'could you please make that, err, **TWO**?'

Kaksi!

Deux!

Two!

Zwei!

To!

Dwa!

Dos!

Dois!

Du..

CHAPTER 6:

HARD WORKER

Suck! **Suuuuck!** **SU-SU-SU-SU!** Suuck! It was all

spotless: the

stairs, kitchen,

living room,

hallway, bedrooms... everything from top to bottom had

been vacuumed and **polished to perfection**.

   'Phew! It's so nice when you see the results of

all your hard work.' 6 took a moment to relax, gazing out

through her sparkling windows to see one of the new

Plane 5s roaring across the sky. 'But before I relax and

have a holiday, I really need to **get a job** now that there's

so many more on offer... Perhaps there's the perfect one

out there for me.'

'Good morning, class,' greeted **24** before glancing at the interactive whiteboard behind her. 'So, we have **3, 5, 2, 0, 1,** and **4** written on the board. Who would like to come up and put these numbers in order?' **71**, who sat next to **29**, had his hand in the air. 'Yes, 71, would you like to try?'

'Can I go to the toilet?' he asked.

'Hmm… In a minute… Hmm… Anyone else have an idea?' asked 24 again. Another hand shot up and flapped. 'Yes, **57**, do you want to have a go?'

'41 just stuck his **finger up his nose** and wiped it under the table…' was her response.

24 sighed. She had just started her job as a teacher, and she was already looking forward to breaking up for the **holidays**.

TERM DATES

SUMMER TERM:
LONG HOLIDAY

6 stood outside School. She had made a list of five potential jobs and her first job was here, in the **role of teacher**. She had been practising hard all morning how to count to 5, and she could even count sbɹɐwʞɔɐq (backwards) if she needed to. As she pressed the buzzer to be let in, she took a deep breath. **'Go for it!'** she thought.

28, the headteacher, greeted her and invited her in. It was a lovely school with **five classes** but 28 wanted it to expand (to whatever the next number would be) to cater for even **bigger** numbers. 28 wanted more and nothing less.

'Good morning, 6, lovely to meet you,' greeted 28 as she smiled, giving 6 a firm handshake.

'Nice to meet you, too,' replied 6, feeling a little nervous.

'Come, let me show you around.' 28 guided 6 through the school, starting with Year 1. After a while they arrived at Year 5.

24 had been waiting for most of the morning for a suitable response from the class. Like earlier, a few numbers had put their hand up. Unfortunately, it was simply to **tell on another number**, to ask to **sharpen their pencil,** or to say that they **felt sick**... Hmm. In order to keep all the class calm, she had decided to take a **brain break.**

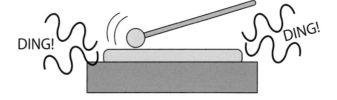

'Hello, 24, I'm here with 6,' announced 28 as she entered the classroom. 'She's come to look around.'

Suddenly, 28 froze as she focused on 24, who was now **half asleep** in her chair.

'**Annnnnnd... Eeeerrrr...** How is your first day going, 24?' asked 28, a little concerned.

'I need a holiday... **now**!' she replied as she quickly took a sip from her coffee flask.

'Perhaps we can all have one tomorrow, but we all need to find the energy to **carry on** until then.' 28 turned to 6. 'So, err, this isn't what it's normally like... So, when would you like your small number to **start school here**?'

6 looked a little confused. **'I came for a job...'** she answered.

'**Ah...** I must have read the **wrong email** or got muddled up,' replied 28, scratching her head. She then glanced down at her phone. 'Ah, my fault, it was 66 who was coming to look around. Anyway, I'm very sorry, 6, but 24 was given the job earlier. There may well be another vacancy soon... but for now, I'm sorry, but all the jobs have been filled.'

6, just like 5 had done yesterday, **steadied her emotions,** despite feeling a little sad. 'Not to worry,' she replied. 'I'll keep my eye out for any future positions. Oh, by the way, the answer to the question on the board is **0, 1, 2, 3, 4,** and then **5.** Or **5, 4, 3, 2, 1,** and then **0,** if you're counting backwards.'

'**Remarkable!**' declared 28. 'You must have **worked hard** to come up with that answer!'

6 pulled out her phone from her pocket,

scrolled through her notes, and looked up the directions to Fl🌸wer Sh🌸p – the second job on her list.

It was a beautiful shop both surrounded and covered, inside and out, by **glorious colourful flowers**. Delightful. As usual, 6 had prepared herself for the interview. She had studied the names of the flowers, as well as having learnt how to take care of them. She was diligent and hardworking. She was ready.

42 TOOK HOLD of the watering can, half filled it with water, and Water (pour onto plants) took it over to the pot. The plant in the pot, instead of standing straight like you would expect, was wilting, **bent over like a banana.**

'This is too much like **hard work**,' thought 42 as he poured only a few drops of water into the dying plant. The dry earth popped and crackled as it quickly soaked up the water, desperate for more. 42 put down the watering can and rubbed his arms. 'I think I'm going to **search for holidays** on the internet instead...'

6 pushed opened the door. A tiny bell that was hung on the back of it announced her arrival.

'Hello!' She paused and waited for a response before repeating her introduction.

30, the owner of Flower Shop, came rushing out from the back of the shop. '**Where are you, 42**? You're supposed to greet our customers and bring out their orders!' she uttered frantically, before locating 42, who was now asleep behind a bunch of daffodils. 'I don't believe it! I'm telling you, you lot of young numbers are **lazy, lazy, lazy!'**

6 moved forward as 30, catching her breath, came over after quickly grabbing a bouquet of flowers.

'You have such lovely **flowers** in your shop,' noted 6, glancing around. 'I see you have **daisies, buttercups, roses,** and **carnations.** Oh, and those lovely **lilies** you have in your hands.'

30 looked a little stunned. 'Oh my, you really know your flowers. You must have **worked hard** to remember all of those! Anyway, sorry for the wait, and here are those **lovely lilies you ordered**,' she added, passing the bunch to 6.

6 stood there, just like she had done at the school, a little confused. 'I haven't ordered any... I've just come for a **job**.'

30 scratched her head before taking a closer look at the card that was stuck within the flowers. **'Oh!'** she gasped, along with an embarrassing **giggle**. 'It actually says these flowers **are for 9** and not for you, 6. I must have

To: 9

Bouquet of flowers

Flower Shop

looked at it **upside down**... that's because I was rushing...'
30 glanced behind her. 42 was now snoring. 'I'm sorry to
say, 6, but 42 was given the job earlier. However, you may
want to try again tomorrow, as things may well have
changed by then. Hmm...'

'No luck. No. Not a chance.' 6 was putting

a cross next to all the jobs she had been to and failed to
get. After Flower Shop, she had **stayed positive**
and had popped into **Phone Shop** and then to
BANK. After being unsuccessful at each, she had
then visited **A i r p o r t**. Despite no offer of a
job, she had impressed everyone she had seen by being
so **dedication** and **determined**. It was unfortunate
that each job she went for had just been given to another
number.

'Not to worry,' she said to herself as she stepped
onto the bus; she had to make her way home to get ready
to go to THE BIG WHITE HOUSE. **'Tomorrow is**
another day to try again.' FIST BUMP MAX!!

peered at her watch. Time was running out – it was nearly time to choose the next **role model**. Chairs still needed to be put out and balloons still needed to be blown up, but unfortunately, only a handful of numbers – apart from 1, 2, 3, 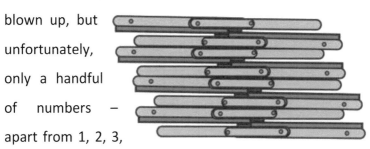 4, and 5 – had shown up early to help.

'I can't wait to see what cakes we have!' boomed **19** excitedly, as he desperately opened up the Five Box and looked inside. 'I don't fancy putting them out... but I *do* fancy eating one!'

'I love balloons!' screeched **46** as she stared at the packets. 'But there's *no way* I'm blowing them up!'

'I need to sit down,' moaned **98**. 'Someone get me a chair as I can't be bothered to get one myself...'

'Hello, 1,' said 6, who was also one of the numbers who had arrived early. 'I see you still have a lot of work to do.'

'Good evening, 6,' replied 1 as he began lifting the chairs off the pile and placing them in front of the house. 'We do. But all the **hard work** is worth it when it's done.' 1 glanced around; it still seemed like there were only a few helping out.

6 smiled, immediately **following 1's example** by taking a chair. 'That's what I always say to myself,' she agreed, putting the chair next to 1's. 'Although I tried hard today, I'm a little disappointed that I didn't get a job. But I'm going to **try again** tomorrow. In fact, I'll try hard every day until I get one.'

The balloons were now fully inflated, the cakes had been put out onto plates (except for the ones that 19 had already taken a bite from), and all the chairs were set out in orderly rows, ready for all the numbers to sit on.

'Good evening,' 0 began, as she glanced out. 'Ah…' She paused, noticing that many numbers were slouching down in their chairs, while some had actually **fallen asleep**. 'Many of you look tired. Have you all been working hard?' she asked.

'I JUST WANT A HOLIDAY!' shouted **42** loudly.

'I don't want to work anymore either,' announced **24**. 'I've worked for a *whole* day… and I also want a long holiday – a **five-day** holiday, in the sun!'

'Well, I can understand. We all need a break, especially when we've been busy. But to continue being **in order** we must continue to **work hard** in helping, volunteering, being thoughtful, and… well… **persevering**, even when things are **tough**.'

Many numbers now sat bolt upright and tried to conceal their yawns behind their hands.

'So,' continued 0, 'we all think that the next role model should help us all by showing us how to be a **hard**

worker, and a number that keeps **persevering**. Now... does any number know such a number?'

It was no surprise that some hands (including the other role models) were immediately raised.

'**I do!**' announced 28 from **School** .

'**Yes! Yes!**' shouted 30 from Flower Shop .

'**Absolutely!**' exclaimed 60 from **Phone Shop** .

'**Certainly!**' shared 50 from **BANK** .

'**Definitely!**' declared 81 from Airport.

'**Magnificent!**' expressed 0 delightedly. 'And what number is that?' she asked.

'**6!**' they all agreed. 'It's 6!'

'Amazingly, that's exactly who we all thought too. She has been an exemplary hard worker,' confessed 0.

'I wasn't expecting this,' admitted 6, feeling slightly nervous as she made her way to the front.

'I have something for you, 6,' shared 0 as she pulled out a badge from her pocket. It had something written on the front.

'What does it say?' questioned 6, glancing at the badge that 0 was now pinning to her chest.

'It's for your new job,' 0 replied happily. 'It says

JOB TITLE:

ROLE MODEL!'

'After a **long time** trying, I've finally been given a job,' 6 said ecstatically.

With that, cameras began to click, cakes began to be eaten, and 6 – feeling a little tired after a very busy day – took a moment to rest.

'I'll just try one of those **scrumptious cakes** from the new Five Box,' she said as applause continued to fill the air, 'because I feel that tomorrow is going to be an even busier day for me!'

With that she smiled before popping a **zingy lemon drizzle cake** straight into her mouth – **lovely.**

THINGS TO DO:
Wake up early.
Move next door to 5.
Invite role models for
breakfast.

CHAPTER 7:

HELPFUL

Zzzz... Zzzz... Zzzz... The curtains remained closed and many numbers were still tucked under their blankets, fast asleep. After the celebrations yesterday evening, 0 thought that it may well be a good time to have a break – **a little holiday for all** – so that they'd all have the strength to choose another role model later today.

Sch**oo**l was closed, much to the delight of 24. Flower Shop was also shut. In fact, the only places that were open – apart from C**O**FFEE SH**O**P, which never closed because of the high demand for Numberchinos, Americountos, Numbreros, and now **Countchinos** – was A**i**rpört, and surprisingly, **B**Ⱥ**NK**.

50, the manager of **B̶A̶NK**, had decided to keep it open. **'Time is numbers!'** she stated to her employees. 'We **haven't got time** to rest. We need to count *beyond* 6 straight away so we can have **bigger** and **better** things to do! We need to find the next number to count on, and I can't even wait until later!'

50 was a very determined (and somewhat demanding) number.

Buzz! Buzz! Buzz!

Bleary-eyed, **7** reached out and hit the **'off'** button on his alarm clock. It was 6 o'clock. And, while many numbers dreamt of the beach, having a relaxing drink at **C☕FFEE SH☕P**, or jumping on a plane to a far-flung destination, 7 was getting ready for his new job at **B̶A̶NK**.

He took a quick sip of coffee before having a final glance in the mirror. He always dressed smartly: a well-ironed white shirt, a perfectly tied tie, and a black felt bowler hat. Impeccable.

Grabbing his briefcase, 7 made his way to the bus stop. The streets were quiet, with the only sound coming from his shoes as they **clopped, clopped, clopped** along the dimly lit pavement.

The bus was relatively empty. Only a handful of numbers sat on the seats, and those that did yawned as they gazed at their phones, hypnotised by a new game they were playing.

The bus headed in the direction of

THE BIG WHITE HOUSE

and the newly built houses where 6 had now moved into. As they went past the park, 7 glanced out the window to see a few numbers out jogging and exercising. **'Phew!'** he thought as he gave a little yawn. 'They must all be very fit. I must really **find the time**.'

Talking of time, just then the bus came to a screeching halt. **50** – who was waiting on the pavement – had her hand out, frantically waving at it to stop.

'Didn't you see me wave my hand for you to stop?' she questioned, quite crossly to **38**, who was driving the bus. 'Don't you know that I have no time to waste? I need to find the next role model now... not later but **now**!'

50 lived in a house that was even larger and grander than THE BIG WHITE HOUSE. After working at BANK for a while, she had saved enough to buy the biggest (and what she thought was the best) house around, although she wanted it bigger. In the night, **she had phoned 53**, the local builder, and ordered him to build another bedroom. When 53 had left, bleary-eyed, 50 had officially become the first number in the street to have **six** bedrooms (although she would love to have even more).

50 sat down on the bus along with a handful of numbers who also worked for **BANK** . The doors shut and, just as the bus was about to go, **shouting could be heard outside**. **8** and **9** were running towards the bus, clearly upset.

'Please help us,' sobbed **8** as he looked up towards the windows of the bus. 'Our ball has got stuck in a tree and we can't get it down. **We need some help**!'

9, who was standing beside him, turned and pointed to the large oak tree. There, up in one of the higher branches, was their ball, far out of reach.

50 immediately reacted. She had **no** time to stop. **No** time to wait. And, certainly, **no** time, whatsoever, to help *little* numbers. '***Move*** it, driver!' she commanded 38. 'We can't stop any longer for them. They can go and help themselves as far as I'm concerned.'

However, just as the bus was about to continue its journey, 7 stood up. 'Please wait. **I will help them**,' he offered kindly.

50 gave 7 one of her famous stares, unimpressed with his response.

'Remember, 7, you work for me! You better not be late as we need to find the next number to count on. I haven't got time today for *little* things. We have **bigger** and **better** things to do!'

The bus pulled away as 7, along with 8 and 9, walked in the direction of the large oak tree. They all gazed high up at the branches that, like a hand, firmly grasped the ball.

'**Hmm....** it's quite a way up but I think we can get it,' said 7, thinking about how they could all reach it. 'Perhaps we could use teamwork like 3 has shown us... but I'll need to **take my hat off** first...'

8 and 9 just stood there, grateful for any suggestions but a little unsure of the plan.

There was a slight wobble, then a little **shake**, before 9 managed to steady himself. 'Oh, my,' quivered 9, balancing himself. 'It's higher up here than it is down there!' 9 glanced back down to 8, who was leaning back slightly, peering up.

'You're doing **great,** 9!' encouraged 7 as he held on tightly to 9's feet. 9 was currently **standing on 7's head** (which was perfect for this sort of thing as it was high off the ground and very flat).

'Steady, steady,' guided 8 as 9 reached high into the air and, with his fingers **stretched** to their fullest, managed to get the tip of one of his nails to scrape the bottom of the ball. However, the ball barely moved.

'Try this.' 7 passed 9 a stick.

9 took it and tried again, this time with success!

'We did it! We did it!' shouted 8 as 9 carefully made his way down off 7's head, following the direction of the ball, which was now by 8's feet.

'Thank you, thank you!' exclaimed 9 ecstatically. 'You've been such a *big* help to us!'

'No problem,' replied 7, a little shyly, as he picked up his briefcase and popped his hat back on his head. 'I enjoy doing **little things to help**.'

7 walked briskly. His legs frantically **flip-flapped**, while his feet **clopped, clopped, clopped** on the pavement, at twice their usual pace. He should still be able to make it to **BANK** on time.

He quickly turned, making his way down a small alleyway near **Phone Shop**. As he did, he bumped into **53** carrying a very **long ladder**.

'Good morning, 53,' said 7, slightly out of breath. 'You're up early. **Aren't you having a holiday**?' he asked.

'Well,' began 53, as he lowered the long ladder, his pot of paintbrushes, and his toolbox, which he was also carrying, to the floor, 'I'm **self-employed**, which means that if I don't work then I don't earn any money.' He sighed. 'I was working at 50's house earlier and now I'm off to School as 28 wants another classroom built – a **sixth** one!'

'You're really following **6's example** of being a hard worker,' commented 7, 'but carrying all those things, and working on your own, can't be easy.'

53 shook his head. 'It's not. No one wants to help, either. Not long ago, I tripped and dropped everything on the floor just as a bus arrived. Many numbers from **BANK** got off, but none of them offered to help. They said that they had **bigger and better** things to do.'

Knowing he might be late for work, but seeing that **53 needed help**, 7 kindly lent a hand. 'I'll help,' offered 7. 'I can carry the long ladder for you.'

Soon, 7's bowler hat was under his arm, and – in exchange – the ladder was sitting, perfectly balanced, on his head.

'You're made for it!' commented 53 with a grin as they began to march down the road. 'Thank you so much for your help.'

7 sat at his desk next to 16, wiped his brow, and took a very deep breath. He didn't know how, but he had just made it on time.

It was frantic in the office. Numbers were busy searching the internet, making phone calls, and sending out posts on social media in order to find **the next number to count on.**

As 7 tapped away on his laptop, searching for big numbers to do the job, 50 and some other colleagues assembled together. 50 had grown tired of waiting and was off to see 0 at **THE BIG WHITE HOUSE** . She wanted to see if they could have the meeting earlier than this evening to choose the next number.

'We want bigger! We want more!' she chanted. 'It's time for a change.' Other numbers raised a banner in the air. ***Bigger is better*** it said in bold letters. 'Let's go and see 0. We have no time to waste! The rest of you, stay here and keep looking!'

'Bigger! Better! Bigger! Better! Bigger! Better!'

The banners were waved in the air as the crowd from

B𐀀NK gathered around the white picket fence. 'We do not have time to waste!' they all shouted. 'We need to find the next role model, **now**!'

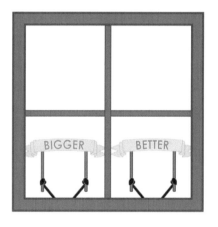

0 glanced out of her front window. 'Hmm, I wonder what's going on?' she pondered as she turned

back to 3 and 5, who had joined her earlier for a cup of tea. 'There seems to be a lot of **commotion** out there.'

Slowly, 0 opened the door and looked out.

'Bigger! Better! Bigger! Better!' the chanting continued.

'Hello everyone,' greeted 0 as she stepped out. 'You all have a lot of energy, and… err… it appears you have come to **tell me something**?' she asked.

'We have!' answered 50, quite abruptly. 'We want to know who the next role model is… *now*! We want to count to more so we can do bigger and better things.'

'Hooray!' cheered the other numbers from BANK. **'More! More! More!'**

'Hmm,' thought 0, as 3 and 5 also joined her. 'Well, it's **not** just about counting in order that… well… counts, but being able to be counted on to be… well… how shall I say it? **Better behaved**. Perhaps you could all come in and join me for a lovely cup of tea. On beautiful days like this it's the little things like having **time for your**

friends and enjoying their company which is the thing that **counts the most**.'

50 looked a little shy. 'Oh, well, actually... I wouldn't mind a cup of tea, as all that marching has made me rather thirsty. And, err, perhaps... if you have any spare... a **lovely slice of cake**, too?' she asked, now a little more relaxed.

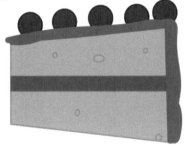

Crowds had now gathered, everyone refreshed and energised from their day off. Many had spent the day at the beach or even at the park, relaxing with friends. Games had been played, picnics had been enjoyed, and the sun had been shining. All in all, it had been a **glorious day for all.**

'Good evening,' began 0 with a smile. 'I can see you've all had a great holiday and I know you've all been doing some amazing things in our lovely town. In order to continue making our town better, we need more than bigger and better things – we need **great numbers** to count on. It doesn't matter how **big** or **small** you are, we can **all** make a difference. And sometimes it's the **little things** we do that can make the **biggest changes**. So, we were wondering if any of you knew of a number who has helped you today and made your day a little better?' she asked, looking out at the crowd.

Immediately, 8 and 9 raised their hands, followed quickly by 53. **'We do!'** they expressed. Slowly, other hands were raised as well.

'WE DO, TOO.' It was 50 and the other numbers from **BANK** .

'Incredible! And what number is this?' 0 enquired, feeling a little excited.

'It's 7!' they shouted together, followed by cheers.

7 looked up as **The Numbers** stood, clapping and appreciating his efforts. 'Why, thank you... but I

simply enjoyed being helpful. It was really no effort,' he replied, turning from his usual **orange** to a **shade of red**.

7 came to the front and stood next to 6.

'Even though you are a small number,' expressed 0, patting him on the back, 'you've shown us how to be in better order and you've made our lives a lot better.' 7 smiled. 'But to celebrate, I feel we need to *go big*...' added 0. It was then that a **giant cake** appeared. 'Sometimes, bigger *is* better,' she giggled.

A large amount of numbers in the crowd also agreed... before they **fainted out of excitement** at the incredibly scrumptious sight before them.

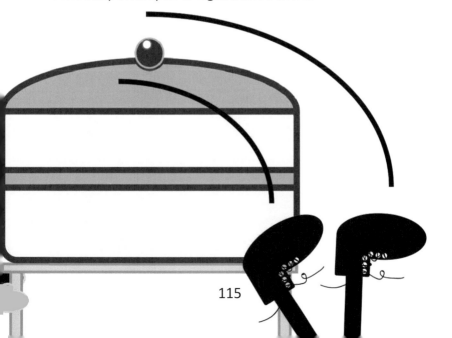

115

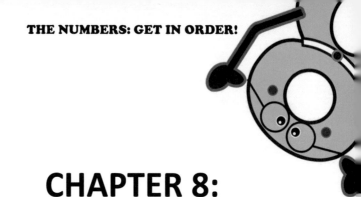

CHAPTER 8:

OPEN-MINDED

Apart from yesterday's holiday, The Numbers, in general, had a daily **routine**: wake up, work, choose a role model, repeat. Many were glad to be back into the swing of things. Some numbers didn't like changing this routine. Some numbers just didn't like change at all. For many, trying anything new at all was a

no,

no,

no!

'Coffee please, 14,' said **77**, 'and make it my **usual**... obviously.' 77 smiled before glancing at his usual seat by the window, overlooking Town Road.

'Would you like it made with extra strong coffee instead?' asked 14.

'No, thank you.'

'How about some **chocolate sprinkles** on the top?'

'No.'

117

'Perhaps you want to try a **Countchino** today?'

'No.'

'In an extra **big cup**?'

'No.'

'How about...'

'No! No! No!' shouted 77 before taking a deep breath. '**Pl-eeea-se**, *just* my **usual**.' As 77 tried his best to stay calm, he noticed that his regular seat had just been taken. **80** was now sitting in it, staring out on the shoppers passing by. **'I don't believe it!'** he cried. 'My seat, which I have *every day*, now has 80 sitting in it!'

8 glanced at the breakfast list on the board. 'Hmm,' he thought as 77 grabbed his coffee and stormed over towards a couple of empty chairs that faced away from the window.

'Would you like your regular?' asked 14, as she immediately went to take 8's usual choice – **a crumpet** – from a plate on the counter.

'Hmm… Actually, I think I'll have **something different**,' he replied.

14, as well as the other numbers in C⬤FFEE SH⬤P, froze.

'Err… something *different*?' she asked, still slightly surprised at 8's reply.

'Yes please. I think I'll have **a change**,' he confirmed. 'I'm doing things a little **differently** today. What would you suggest?'

'*Me?*' asked 14, again feeling a little shocked. 'Not many numbers ask *my* opinion.' 14 then turned her eyes to something else. 'Hmm… How about a lovely **toasted sandwich**, then?'

'Ooh, I've never tried that before. What a good idea!'

8 glanced around. Nearly every seat was taken, all except one – the one next to 77, who was still upset about not getting his usual seat.

Along with his toasted sandwich, 8 sat down next to him. **'Ooh, lovely!'** he remarked as he bit into his crispy, crunchy toastie.

77, looked up, somewhat in disgust. 'I don't like to try anything new…' he muttered, glancing down into his Americounto. **'I know what I like, and I like what I know.'**

'Well, it's only today that I thought I'd **do things differently**,' began 8 as he reflected back on his morning. 'It all began with my usual YOGA session and then a new move – **a handstand!** It was then that I saw things differently and started **looking at things in another way**…'

77 popped his coffee back onto the table and turned his head upside down. 'Hmm, they do indeed! Oh, apart from **one thing**…' he commented with a little grin.

'What's that?' asked 8, slightly baffled.

'You!' he chuckled. 14, overhearing the conversation, also giggled.

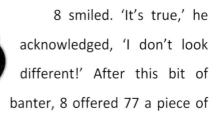

8 smiled. 'It's true,' he acknowledged, 'I don't look different!' After this bit of banter, 8 offered 77 a piece of his toastie. 'Please, try a bit,' he offered.

Tentatively, 77 **took it**, **sniffed it**, and then slowly **put it into his mouth** and chewed. 'Mmm! This is **amazing**!'

'It's very nice, isn't it?' agreed 8. 'I've decided to spend a day trying things that I haven't tried before.'

'Hmm,' pondered 77. 'You know, I may just do the same.'

A new development was going to be built in the park – a **state-of-the-art** running track. **78**, from CouNt Modern, had designed it and he cared deeply about the way it **looked**. He was working with **53**, who only cared if it was **practical** and that it worked properly.

'**Nah!** It won't work. It's **not practical** having it go in this direction,' stated 53, shaking his head.

Plans For Running Track

Track

'Well, that's the **new** design, which **looks** amazing,' replied 78 sternly, as he held up the plan to the track. '*See*… it looks *so* much better if the track goes this way…'

There was a clear difference of opinion, and it also seemed they were still learning the lesson about teamwork that 3 had taught them. They were struggling to see **eye to eye**, and perhaps they were still learning to be **open-minded** to each other's idea.

'I've been doing this for *years*,' boasted 53 as he picked up his hammer. 'A running track must *always* go **left**.'

'That's so prehistoric, ancient, from the **Dark Ages**,' 78 replied, somewhat sarcastically. 'Nowadays, in these *modern* times, it doesn't. It goes **right**... just like in *my* amazing design.'

8, now feeling full up from eating his delicious toastie, turned in the direction of the park to have a little exercise. As he did, he **stumbled** upon **53** and **78**.

'Good morning, both of you,' greeted 8 as 53 and 78 turned around. It was clear by the expressions on both of their faces that the morning wasn't that good.

'What would *you* choose?' began 78 straight away as he flapped the plan

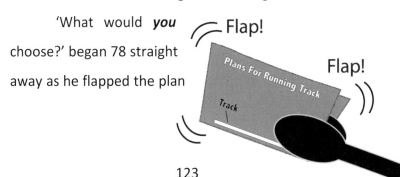

in front of 8's face. 'Left, or *right*?'

'Well... sorry, what?' 8 enquired, a little baffled.

'*Left* is the way it should go, 78. It won't work otherwise,' responded 53 abruptly. 'Trust me, it simply won't!'

'Sorry, **what** needs to go left or right?' 8 asked again, still unsure.

'A running track!' they both answered as 78 gave 8 the plan.

8 looked at it carefully. 'Hmm, if you look at the plans this way, then you will naturally have to run **left**... but if you look at it another way, then you will naturally have to run **right**. This means that both your ideas are... the **same**! Both 78 and 53 looked at each other, slightly stunned. 'I have another idea, though...'

To their delight, 8 helped them see things a little differently, and came up with another plan – one that used both 78 and 53's ideas.

'This design should work,' admitted 53, grabbing his screwdriver from his pocket.

'Oh my,' began 78, looking at the new plan in awe. 'This does look rather amazing. You can run **left**, run **right**, or even in a **circle**! Who would have thought that a running track could be made as a circle? **Incredible**!'

TING! Just as 8 was about to leave, a notification came in on their phones.

'Oh, there has been a **change of plan**...' noted 53, reading a message from 0. 'It seems we're no longer having the meeting at THE BIG WHITE HOUSE. Instead, it'll be at the new *Dance Club* later on, to celebrate it opening...'

'Well, the building looks amazing, obviously, as **I designed it**,' added 78 with a swish of his hair. 'However, I've heard they're still working on their dance routine, which may not be *quite* as good... That's all I'm saying...'

Boom! Boom! Boom! Shake! Shake! Shake! Boom! Boom! Boom! Shake! Shake! Shake!

went the music as **37** added his own style of dancing at **Dance Club**.

'Why are you **shaking**, 37?' giggled **36**. 'Are you cold? Hee-hee! You should be trying *my* idea — **twisting**!'

'What? Why are you both shaking and twisting?' huffed **74** as she began to rotate. '*My* idea is far better — you should be spinning instead!'

It was clear that the three of them weren't going to try any ideas apart from their own. Just as the music was about to be played again, 8 — having said goodbye to 78 and 53 — decided to pop in to see how their routine was going.

'Good afternoon,' began 8 as he took a look around, before moving through the rows of chairs towards the stage where 36, 37, and 74 were practising their moves. 'This looks like fun. I would love to dance like you all.'

'Perhaps *just* like me...' responded **37** as he began to shake.

'Definitely *not* like him,' laughed **36**, 'but absolutely like *me*.'

'Stop! Stop! Stop!' demanded **74**. 'Please, don't embarrass yourselves. We all know that *I'm* the one with the **best** idea **and** the best move. 8, **this** is how you dance.'

'Actually,' began 8 as he clapped his hands, appreciating all their effort. 'They **all look great**. I can't wait to try each of your ideas and watch your routine later.'

'Hmm,' they all replied together, a little surprised. 'We've **never tried** each other's ideas before, and our routine... well... it isn't quite finished.'

'Oh,' replied 8, surprised that they hadn't tried. 'Well, today I decided to try new things and, so far, it's made my day really fun! Why don't we try and make a routine together? I'm sure it would be amazing!'

Boom! Shake! Boom! Twist! Boom! Spin! thumped the music. 36, 74, 37, and 8 began to put their ideas and dance moves together.

'Wow!' they exclaimed, slightly surprised at how it had all turned out. 'This is an amazing routine! We should have tried each other's ideas before!'

'I do have one idea myself, if you'd like to try it?' suggested 8. 'And this move means you'll be looking at things **very differently** than before...' he giggled. 'It'll be so much fun to do later in front of the other numbers!'

37, 36, and 74 all looked at each other. 'Hmm, **let's do it**!' they all agreed.

'Oh,' sighed **22** as she shuffled along the rows of chairs. 'I'm not expecting it to be too good. Look at the way the numbers from *Dance Club* dress.' 22 lifted up her new designer sunglasses to have a proper look, then sniggered.

'I know, 22,' replied **51**, her friend, as she stuck her nose in the air. 'They look a little boring... not like us.'

'I couldn't agree more,' added **75**, another friend, as they sat down, facing the stage. 'To be honest, I'm not too happy we're here. I have **my routine**, and I'd much prefer to be at The Big White House , if I'm honest.'

● leapt up onto the stage as the lights above began to dazzle down. **'Good evening,'** she began. 'Firstly, sorry for changing your routines tonight and asking you to come here instead to celebrate the opening of **Dance Club** . I know we all like to have a routine, but being open to **new ideas** can make our day a little more fun! So, I hope we're going to have fun by watching **Dance Club** and their **amazing dance routine**!'

Boom! Boom! Shake! Shake! Boom! Boom! Twist! Twist! Boom! Boom! Spin! Spin! went the music as 36, 37, 74, and 8 took to the stage. It was **incredible**, with **shakes** and **twists**, and **spins** galore. Then, just when you thought it couldn't get any better, a **new move** was introduced – one that had never been seen before.

8 took centre stage before, suddenly, as all the audience **held their breath**... **Flip!** 8 and the other numbers were in a

. Amazing!

'Oh my!' gasped 22, 51, and 75 as they looked on. 'We weren't expecting it to be this good!'

There was a giant

as 0 and the other role models also came up on stage to congratulate them. **'That was simply amazing!'** exclaimed 0 joyfully. 'Well done!'

As **Dance Club** began to leave the stage, 0 asked 8 to remain. 'As I mentioned, it can be good to be

open-minded to new ideas and to new ways of doing things. There are times when we need to look at things in another way, and I'm not just talking about doing an amazing handstand to see things differently! I'm talking about seeing things from **another number's point of view**, especially when they have different ideas to ours. So, I think it'll be good to have the next number to **count on** as a number who is open-minded. What do you all think?' she asked. 'And **what number** should it be?'

Numbers **shared ideas**, **listened**, and took other **opinions** on board before coming up with an answer. 'We know!' they all shouted. **'It's 8!'**

'Just what we thought, too!' announced 0, with a grin.

'Ooh!' giggled 8. 'It was never in my mind that I'd ever be chosen!'

As the music played and **Dance Club** again took to the stage, many numbers tried to be open-minded and copy 8's incredible handstand. Well, 66 took a **little convincing** to try one – he was worried that his

secretly hidden Seven Box would fall out of his pocket if he did.

He was right to be cautious; when it eventually did fall out, 88 was not open-minded to 66's idea of **not** telling her his secret. **Oh dear...**

CHAPTER 9:

PATIENCE

3 passed a little biscuit to 4.

'Ooh, I never thought by looking at them that this would taste so delicious!' responded 4. 'Very tasty indeed.'

All the role models were sitting around the table in 0's kitchen, gathering their thoughts and thinking of the past week.

'Isn't it strange, in a funny way, that we're all **the smallest ones**?' noted 5 while taking a nibble himself.

'Well,' began 0, 'you weren't chosen because of your size but by the **great examples** you set.'

133

'It's lovely that we count in order up to 8 but, more importantly, that we're all learning from each other how to be in better order,' added 2. 'We've all come a long way from... well...' she giggled as she turned to face 0, **'from nothing!'**

8 was sitting, quietly sipping his tea, staring out of the window. His thoughts were temporarily elsewhere. He missed his friend. His small friend. The only little number **who hadn't been chosen**.

'What's up?' asked 7 as he shifted onto the seat next to him. 'You don't seem to be your usual self.'

'Thank you for asking,' replied 8, turning back to the room. 'I was just thinking of my friend, **9**. He's a **small number** like us but he hasn't been chosen. He's such a good number, too.'

'Well, we need **more numbers** to count on. I'm sure he'll be chosen soon,' replied 7.

'We do,' agreed 0, overhearing the conversation. 'However, it could be a **long time** until every number is in order. I feel many numbers will have to learn to be **patient** for their turn...'

9 was relaxing on one of the benches in the park. He had just been to Phone Shop and was now glancing down at his new prized possession – **Phone 8**: a phone so advanced, you could even use it **upside down**. Incredible! Unfortunately, it wasn't connecting to the internet properly and he wanted to check his bank balance to see how much money he had left after buying the phone.

'Hmm, it's still not working,' sighed 9. 'Hmm...'

'What?' The question came from **31**, who was sitting on the bench next to him. 'What's wrong with my new phone's internet?' He was clearly getting a little frustrated.

'**Hey!** This is supposed to be a *new* phone and it doesn't even work! What **rubbish**!' shouted **93**, who was a couple of benches further down. He was also distressed, perhaps a little angry. He then flipped it the other way. '**Aaagh!**' he yelled. 'It doesn't even work upside down! I can't *count* on it to work!' Without warning, 93 took his phone and...

Bang!

Crash!

He whacked it on the bench, breaking it into eight pieces.

9 looked around him, noticing how frustrated the other numbers were. **'Let me try again,'** he thought as he heard more **bangs, slaps, shakes,** and **rattles** from other numbers and their phones. 'If it doesn't work, I'll have to go to **BANK** instead,' he sighed.

'I don't know how you stay so **patient**,' remarked 93 as he picked up the broken pieces, noticing 9's **calm composure**. 'I hate it when things don't work.'

'I don't like it either,' replied 9 with a smile, 'but staying **patient** means I **still have a phone**.'

93 glanced at 9's device, and then to his, which was now in pieces. **'That's true,'** 93 sighed.

"HAVING A MEETING – OPENING LATE" it read on the notice that had been stuck on the outside doors of **BANK** . 9 had just

arrived and, like many that were waiting in front of him in the queue, he took a very deep breath.

'Every time I come to **BANK** , it's either shut, opening late, or there are super-long queues...' **62** said, huffing and puffing. 'I **hate** waiting! **Hate it! Hate it! HATE IT!'** she screamed.

' **BANK** always tells you that **time is numbers**...' said **94**, placing her hands on her hips as she shook her head. 'Now they're wasting *my* time. I hope they're going to pay me a lot of numbers for waiting!'

Some numbers didn't fancy sticking around to wait for **BANK** to open and so went home, while others – especially those at the back of the giant queue – stepped out and began to force their way to the front.

'I *need* to go first!' **72** cried while he pushed past everyone else. 'Move it!'

'No, *I* do!' demanded **59**, swinging her handbag in the air like she was a **helicopter**.

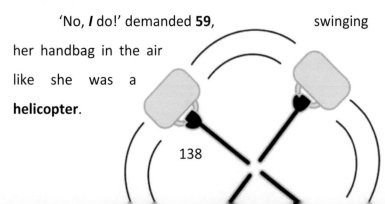

138

Whirl-donk! Whirl-donk! Whirl-donk! went her bag as it knocked into the heads of those who were waiting.

Despite many remaining calm, and some still being kind and caring, a few, notably bigger numbers, 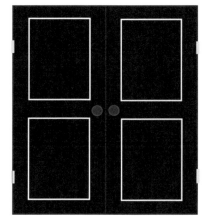 weren't... well... in order. A group of them had gathered at the front, **pushing and pulling, moaning and groaning,** and **knocking and banging** on the doors. It was only when the doors finally opened that they exploded through with a thud, landing in a pile on the floor. As they got up and raced to the front desk, 9 – on the other hand – **walked in patiently.**

When he arrived and was thanked by 16 for being so patient, he was told how much money he had left:

zero, nil, **less than 1, nought,** or more commonly known as... **nothing.**

QUIET AREA - **NO**ISE

---

9 sat down with his cheap coffee near a handful of numbers that had gathered on the neighbouring tables. It was a new **quiet area** where numbers could enjoy their coffee in peace...

'Well, let me tell *you* something...' began **29** as she put down her coffee, ready to tell her story. Surprisingly, she was sitting with her friends in the quiet area. 'I bought the new Phone 8 today, and guess what? **It didn't work**!'

'You can't trust anything to work these days,' added **87**, whose voice rose above 29's.

'I **TOTALLY** agree,' responded **92**, even louder.

"IT'S AWFUL!"

9 opened his eyes. 'Hmm,' he thought, 'they seem quite loud.'

19 was also sitting in the quiet area. He was not impressed with all the commotion and relentless chattering. 'Grr… **can't they read the sign**?' he huffed while picking up his herbal tea. 'Some of us have come here to relax and *not* talk nonsense.'

'And then,' continued 29, as she put a bag from Phone Shop on the table, 'they replaced it with a new phone!'

'Amazing!' remarked 87 loudly.

'INCREDIBLE!' shouted 92.

19 was just about ready to explode; he shook with rage, spilling his tea over the table and floor. **'I've had enough!'** he yelled.

Just as he was about to go over and scream at the numbers, 9 stood up and went to talk to them, quietly.

'Good morning,' said 9 cheerfully. 'It sounds like you're all having an interesting morning, with so much to share. But I thought I'd politely come over to remind you that this is a **quiet area**.'

The numbers turned to him, as 9 continued to smile. **'Oh,'** gasped 29 as she noticed the large sign above her. 'I'm so sorry, it's my fault. I didn't see. I was just very excited to get my phone working again. We'll move straight away.'

As he sat back down, 9 felt a **nudge on his back**. He turned to see 19 by his ear.

'I don't know how you stayed **so patient** with them,' he whispered. 'I was ready to give them a good piece of my mind.'

'It only took me a minute to explain to them,' replied 9, 'and it seems they're happy over there. And I, well… **I still have a coffee to drink**,' he added jokingly.

19 looked back to what was left of his herbal tea, which was now just a large puddle on the floor. 'Hmm, I think **I'll do the same next time**,' he chuckled.

9 took out the last of his money, popped it

into the machine, and pulled out his ticket ready to get on

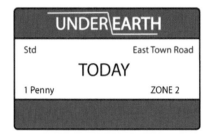

the UNDER\EARTH train – a train that went under the ground to different locations all across town. He was off, like many, to

THE BIG WHITE HOUSE to choose the next number to count on.

'Please stand clear of the closing doors,' echoed the voice on the tannoy. The doors of the busy, stuffy train were starting to close.

9 shuffled further inside as **79**, carrying a large rucksack on his back, quickly squeezed through the closing doors.

'I made it!' he roared with delight.

Bonk! Unfortunately, his bag didn't. The doors, trying to close, knocked against it. The doors then opened again before… **bonk!** Again, they hit the bag.

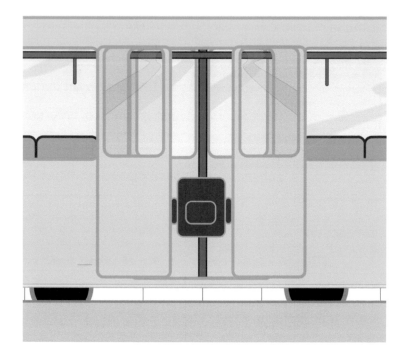

'*Please* remove your items from the closing doors,' instructed **47**, the train driver.

79 just stood there, **unaware** of what was going on as he shoved his headphones over his ears and turned up the music on his new Phone 8. The doors tried to close again. **Bonk!**

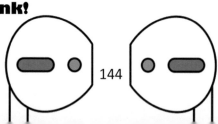

144

'Please, **remove your items** from the doors. Otherwise, the train **cannot** move!' By now 47 was getting a little frustrated, and he wasn't the only one.

'Move out of the way!' shouted **55** angrily.

'Pull your bag out… **NOW**!' screamed **35**.

Bonk! Bonk! Bonk! went the doors, trying their best to close.

9, seeing that 79 wasn't able to hear their commands, politely tapped him on his shoulder. A little bewildered, 79 pulled off his headphones and turned around. **'Sorry, 79,'** said 9 politely. 'Your bag is in the way and the doors can't shut.'

Feeling a little embarrassed, and surprised, 79 eased his rucksack in before… *whoosh!* The doors closed with ease behind him.

'Oops,' he remarked.

'I don't know how you stayed so **patient** with him, I couldn't,' admitted 35, whispering in 9's ear as he removed his blue DAREDEVIL helmet.

'I suppose it's **just practise**, that's all,' smiled 9 in reply.

Along with 0 and the other role model numbers, 8 waited by the white picket fence and glanced out. He was waiting for 9. He hadn't seen him all day and he hadn't been able to contact him on his new Phone 8 either. However, it wasn't long before 9 arrived, along with the other numbers.

'We can't wait any longer,' a handful of numbers moaned, only minutes after they had arrived. 'We've been waiting all day in long queues, and we don't want to wait anymore!'

'Well, I want to go home too and try to **fix my new phone**,' groaned 62 as she gave the phone a little **whack**. 'I don't want to have to wait!'

'Oh dear,' sighed 0. 'I know it can be difficult waiting for something, and no number likes it when things don't work, but we must try to be **patient** now that we're so much busier than before. It's easy to complain

Bye! Bye! Bye! Bye

and get upset when we're stressed, but being **polite and patient** is a good skill to learn.'

Immediately, phones were put down and blushes appeared on faces.

'Well, **I know** a polite and patient number,' shared **16** from **BANK**.

'So do I!' mentioned **35** and **79**, who had been on the train earlier.

'And **we do too**!' added the numbers from CØFFEE SHØP.

'Oh, this is exciting!' exclaimed 0 cheerfully. 'And, to be honest... **I can't wait to hear**! So... what number is that?' she asked.

Suddenly, they all shouted out a name. **'9!'**

8 fell over in shock and excitement hearing that his friend was going to be the next number to count on.

9, however, waited patiently for all the applause and cheers to finish before making his way towards 0 and the other role models. 'Oh my... Can I just say that I wasn't expecting to be **chosen this quickly**!' he admitted with a smile as he helped pick 8 up off the floor.

'Well, I'm so happy that *we* didn't have to wait for **you** any longer. You're such a good number to follow,' admitted 0. 'And, I must say, it's delightful that we now have all you little **Ones** in order, and together. I do hope that all the bigger numbers can finally **be in order**, too, by following your examples.'

'That'll be the day!' shouted **83** as she took a sip of orange juice and went a bit wobbly.

'Oh dear,' remarked 0. '**Oh deary dear**.'

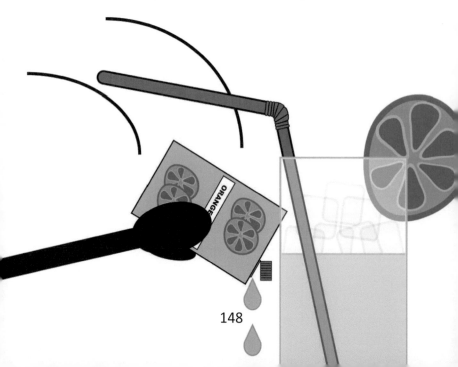

CHAPTER 10:

RESPONSIBLE

'This is so much easier,' thought **13** to himself as he pulled 9's letters out of his bag. 'All the little **Ones** are now **in order** and are so easy to find...'

Despite the bit of order, however, it was soon clear that **not** every number was easy to find.

Next door to 9, 83 still had her curtains closed, and

bottles of juice, tasty treat wrappers, and the occasional crisp packet were piled up outside.

'Hmm, I think we're all **still recovering** from yesterday's party to

149

celebrate 9 being the next number to count on.' 13 looked at the mess for a moment before, suddenly, he felt the whole of his body **shake, twist,** and **turn**. **'Oh!'** he remarked. 'Some **big numbers** aren't quite ready to be in order and are still having a party!'

Boom! Boom! Boom! Boom!

0 peered out of her window. 'Hmm… It seems like many **big numbers** are finding it difficult to follow the little **Ones'** good examples,' she thought. It was then, barely above the noise, that she heard a knock on the door. **It was 1.**

'Good morning, O!' shouted 1 as he placed his

fingers in his ears. 'Can you hear that!' 0 nodded before quickly inviting him in. 'I don't think all the big numbers are in order,' commented 1, now in a quieter voice.

'Funny, I had a feeling yesterday evening that some were still… well… learning too,' replied 0, thinking of what to do. 'Perhaps we can **message** all the **big numbers**. I feel we need a **big responsible number** for

them all to follow. Perhaps then we can ***all*** be in order…
finally!'

> From: 0
>
> To: **1 , 2 , 3 , 4 , 5 , 6 , 7 , 8 , 9 , 99 , 68 , 70**
>
> We're after a big responsible number
> to follow the little **Ones.**
> Meeting tonight
> @ The Big White House – 0.

Ping! 10 looked down at his phone. Email:
We're after a big responsible number to follow the little
Ones. Meeting tonight at The Big White House – 0.

'**Hmm… Interesting,**' he thought before glancing
back up and out of his kitchen window. 'I see what 0
means,' he added, noticing a group
of **big numbers** who were acting a
little silly, bumping into lamp posts
and running around after eating too
many tasty treats from the party last
night. He then glanced at the abandoned

litter that was scattered everywhere. 10 also heard some rather naughty language too. 'Hmm,' he pondered again.

'I can't follow *little* Ones!' shouted **92** as he thumped accidentally into a brick wall.

'Me neither!' agreed **69** at the top of her voice. 'We're too big!'

'I'm going to be the next role model,' screeched **26** while shoving a whole chocolate cake into her mouth. **"BOU 'AN 'AWL 'OLLOW 'I E-AMPLE"** (You can all follow my example). Half the cake that had been **jammed** into her mouth had now been sprayed onto 47 who, a moment earlier, had been laughing at her.

'Hey! I'm never going to follow you!' he blustered, looking down at his cake-stained t-shirt. 'I should be the next role model as I have an important and *responsible* job driving the UNDER\EARTH trains... although I don't really feel like going to work today...'

10 sighed as he glanced back down at his email. 'I think I'm going to help 0 try to find the **big responsible**

role model we need.' With that, he popped his phone in his pocket, took his house keys off the kitchen table, and headed out in search of the next **big thing** – a big number they could all count on.

10 was trying his luck as he walked eastwards along Town Road. Like he usually did, he took a moment to pick up several pieces of stray rubbish that were blowing around his feet. Then he stopped outside Flower Shop and looked inside. 'Hmmm, perhaps there's a responsible number **in here**,' he thought.

Similar to the day when 6 had visited, 42 was slumped up against the counter. **TING!** went the bell to the shop as 10 stepped in and looked around. 42 slowly lifted his head, shook it, and put it back down again. 30 had gone on holiday a couple of days ago (the day 7 was chosen as a role model) and was returning later today. She was staying with her **half and quarter cousins** in another town and was enjoying her time there. This meant that 42 now ran the shop.

'Err... Hmm,' thought 10 as he noticed all the dry and shrivelled plants. 'I wonder if there are any responsible numbers in here.'

Eventually, as 10 approached, 42 responded. **'Morning,'** he groaned. 'I need to go back to bed. I still have music ringing in my ears.'

'Err... the plants look a little dry,' 10 expressed. 'Are you going to water them?' he asked.

'Me?' he replied, a little surprised. 'No. 30 told me to **look after the shop**. She didn't say anything about looking after the **flowers**...'

10 scratched his head, a little confused. 'Err...' He was about to explain to him that looking after the shop *actually* meant being responsible for the flowers, too. However, he simply smiled and decided to help 30 by **watering the plants himself**.

Suddenly the door to the shop opened. **TING!** It was 30.

'Ah, what a lovely time I've had,' she began, full of vigour. 'I've had such an am-' Suddenly, she came to an abrupt stop. **'What's happened?** All my plants look like they're dying!'

42 quickly wiped the sleep from his eyes. **'Err…'**

30 just stared at him in disbelief.

'Don't worry, I've just given them a little water,' began 10 with a smile. 'I think they'll be **OK in a while**.'

30 turned to him in relief. 'Oh, 10. **Thank you! Thank you! Thank you!** I think you're the big **responsible** number we've been looking for… Isn't he, 42? Hmm…'

Science Park

was a new set of buildings, where numbers could share interesting ideas and where amazing products could be created (all inspired by 8's open-mindedness).

Feeling eager, 10 peered through the buildings' windows, fascinated to see what was being made. He was also a little excited, as he thought that there may well be a big responsible number working inside.

Lights from machines flashed, and bright fluorescent liquids bubbled and frothed in nine rows of tall test tubes as 10 entered the large open-plan building.

'**Don't press that, 49!**' cried **32**, the chief scientist who worked there. 'Don't you press that button either, 70!' It was too late. 70 and 32 had just pressed it – the button that **launched** the new **Plane 9** into the air.

LAUNCH

Both 49 and 70 looked at each other, confused. 'We were only after our **lunch**,' they replied, rubbing their empty stomachs.

'Lunch?' repeated 32. 'That button doesn't say lunch... It says l-**A**-u-n-c-h! **LAUNCH**!' 32 froze as the engines started and the plane that sat at the back of the large room began to move. 'We need to stop it, **now**!' he cried.

Strolling over, and still in awe of the newly built creations around him, 10 noticed the commotion.

'Someone stop that plane!' yelled 32 again.

10 turned, seeing the plane edge further and further away from the take-off stand. 'Hmm, I think that's the plane they're talking about,' he thought to himself.

The other numbers were in a panic, desperately trying to find the stop button. As they did, they bumped into the test tubes – **spilling the liquid** they contained all over the floor as well as **breaking important machines** that had taken days to build.

10 quickly walked over to the take-off stand. There, in bright red, was a button with the word **STOP** on

it. He reached out and pressed it. Within an instant, Plane 9 came to an abrupt halt.

'Thank you, thank you, 10!' cheered 32 as he rushed over. 'At last, a responsible number!'

10 blushed. 'Hello, 32, that's fine,' he responded politely. 10 then glanced around the building, still in wonder at what he saw. 'It's amazing what you're all doing here. There's so many exciting things to see.'

'Well, that's really all thanks to 8, whose open-minded ideas got us started,' stated 32 as he caught his breath. 'However, as you've probably noticed, we're **still learning** how to use all the new equipment...'

As he was about to elaborate further, the chief designer, **84** – who was over by the new coffee machine along with 78 from CouNt Modern – started to throw a **TANTRUM** =

'Why isn't this new, super-modern machine working? Who is *responsible* for putting water and coffee in it?' she screamed.

'It doesn't have either!'

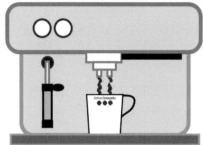

'Err, and some of us,' continued 32 with a shrug of his shoulders, 'are still learning to be responsible.'

'Oh dear,' sighed 10, a little disappointed. 'I was hoping to find a big responsible role model here.'

It was getting late, and still 10 hadn't found the next big thing. He had tried all across town in various shops, factories, and restaurants, as well at the airport, the bank, and anywhere else he could think of, but it seemed that the big numbers **were struggling** to be in order. They were finding it hard to follow the little **Ones'** great examples.

PING! 10 pulled out his phone from his pocket. Email: ***Meeting starting in five minutes. Hopefully we've found a responsible role model – 0.*** 10 shook his head. 'I've really tried,' he sighed. 'I really hope we can find a number that **the big numbers can follow**. Otherwise, not only are we never going to count to anything bigger, but we're also never going to be in order either...'

> From: 0
> To: 1 , 2 , 3 , 4 , 5 ,
>
> Meeting starting
> Hopefully we've
> responsible role

10 moved across to THE BIG WHITE HOUSE . The little **Ones** were ready, waiting eagerly in front of it, to see what big number would step forward to help the bigger numbers get in order after them.

10 smiled and took his seat as 0, ready to address the rather large audience, waited for things to settle down. It was clear that some big numbers were still having a few problems following the little **Ones'** examples.

'I don't know what it is,' cried **67** while shaking her head, 'but I'm struggling to follow the little **Ones'** examples.'

'Me too!' sobbed **46** with her head in her hands, 'It's not about the way they look, it's just... well... I need bigger help!'

Other big numbers agreed with her feelings.

'Good evening, everyone,' began 0 as she nodded, understanding what the big numbers were feeling. 'Yes, that's why we thought it would be a good idea if you had bigger help, as many of you are still struggling to follow the little **Ones'** great examples. So, did any of you manage to find a **big responsible number** at all?' she asked.

There were a few whispers and nods of heads.

'Well, a responsible number **watered my flowers when I was away,'** spoke **30**. 'Although, it wasn't a number who worked at the shop...' 30 turned to 42 who was beside her. 'Hmm...'

'I noticed a responsible number, too,' mentioned **32** from Science Park . 'While many numbers pressed buttons they shouldn't do, this number managed to **fix the problem,** avoiding the premature launch – not lunch – of the new Plane 9.'

'**I did too,**' mentioned **28** from School .

'**And me,**' added **50** from BANK.

'So, what number was so responsible?' 0 enquired.

'**10!**' they answered with a cheer.

'Well, it seems we have the big responsible number we can count on! So, **10 will follow the little Ones** and be the first of, well, the **Tens**!' declared 0 as again, the big numbers – now excited to have a number like them to follow – continued to applaud.

10 just sat there, almost speechless, before being encouraged to stand next to 0. 'I was just doing what **needed to be done**, that was all,' he spoke humbly.

THE TENS!

Suddenly, **64** called out. **'But what order am I in?'** I'd like to be counted on too!' she said, scratching her head.

'And us!' Other big numbers also raised the question.

'Well, you can all be **great examples** to follow by showing how **orderly** and **well behaved** you are. But, as we all know, we also need to **count in order** too! So,' pondered 0, 'all big numbers are made of two parts, a **big** part and a **small** part. Perhaps it makes sense that these parts follow the same order as the **Ones**.' 0 turned to 1 and asked him over. 'If 1 stands next to me and I stay here where the **Ones** are, we make…?'

'10!' cried the bigger numbers.

'Of course! And if **I move out of the way** and we imagine another **1 in my place**, we have number…?' questioned 0, as many bigger numbers – counting their fingers and toes, and whatever else they could find – tried to work out the answer.

'**Oh my,**' gasped **11**, feeling a little dizzy after doing the calculation. 'You have **me**!'

'And, following the order of **Ones**, when 1 is replaced by 2...' continued 0.

'**We have me!**' cried **12**, feeling equally excited.

Soon, more numbers were in order all the way to 19.

'But what happens now? **Who is after 19**?' asked the rest of the numbers.

'Don't worry,' 0 replied with a smile. 'There is room for all of us. If we change one **Ten** to two **Tens**, we will have...' 2 quickly rushed forward and stood next to 0.

'**Me!**' shouted **20**, ecstatically.

'We then count in order like before,' added 0. 'So, we will have 21, 22, 23, and so on...'

Within a few moments, numbers from 0 to 10, and from 10 all the way to 99, were standing in line.

HOORAY!

It was then that a booming voice was heard far in the distance. 'And I'm first of the **HUNDREDS**!' **100** called out in glee.

'Now,' sighed 0, deeply, 'we are all *finally* in order in the way we can count – without getting into a muddle.'

Upon hearing the news, 13 simply collapsed from overexcitement. 66 also felt a little giddy at the thought of making the Hundred Box of cakes.

'However,' continued 0 as the big numbers began to shuffle themselves into order, 'the **most important thing** we have all recently learnt, apart from being able to count, is to be **great numbers to count on**. We all have the ability to be **amazing role models**, no matter what shape or size we are.'

There were continued cheers of delight as **The Numbers** stood, while having the best party ever, in the most amazing **orderly line** you could possibly imagine... **just like they still do today.**

HOORAY!

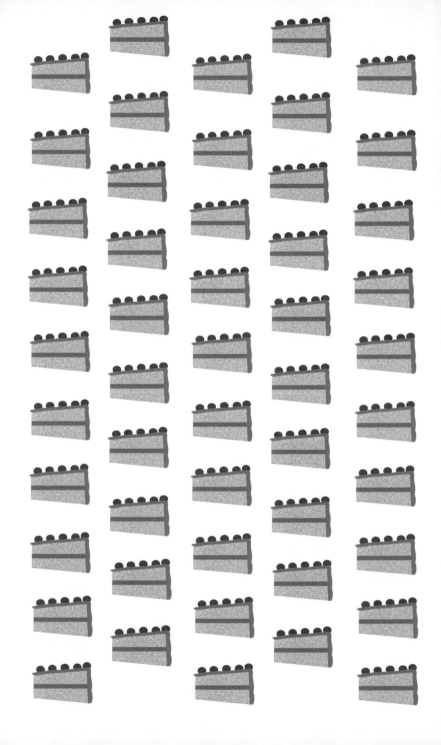

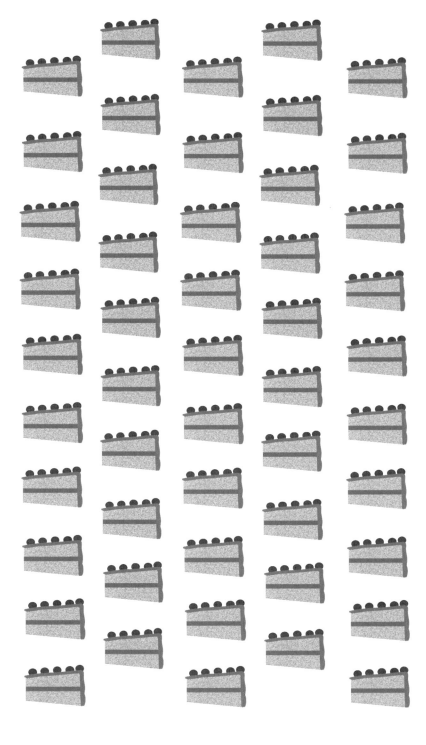

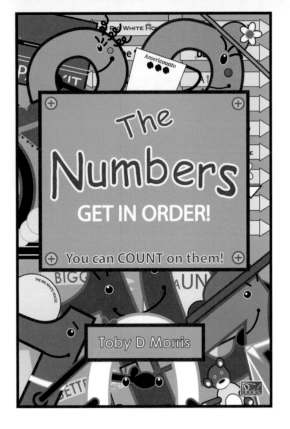

ISBN: 9781909286870

THE NUMBERS:
GET IN ORDER!

It's true. In this **first book** of the series **The Numbers** weren't in order. Not only could they not count but they couldn't be counted on at all – they simply weren't very well-behaved! Find out how **The Numbers** – with the help of some outstanding **ROLE MODELS** – got in order, were able to count, and most importantly became well-behaved **Numbers** you could **COUNT** on!

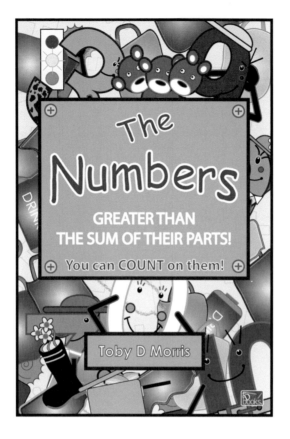

ISBN: 9781909286320

THE NUMBERS:
GREATER THAN THE SUM OF THEIR PARTS!

Bad gas was one of the problems, but that wasn't related to **The Numbers**' new plant-based diets... it had been building for a while. Now faced with an **environmental catastrophe**, **The Numbers** need to come together and be **greater than the sum of their parts** to reverse the possible disaster before it's too late. Can they be **counted** on to work together and get the job done in this **second book** of the series? Well, if anyone can, it's **them!**

ISBN: 9781909286337

THE NUMBERS:
A FRACTION OF THEIR POTENTIAL!

The Fractions - distant cousins of **The Numbers** - had never really experienced doing anything **wholly**: just half a job here, a quarter of the effort there. However, along with their **half-hearted** ways, many were **afraid** to experience life to the **full**. So, in this **third book** of the series, when they come to visit, 0 and the other role models set out a plan... to help **The Fractions** expand their old **mind-sets** and live up to their **whole potential!**

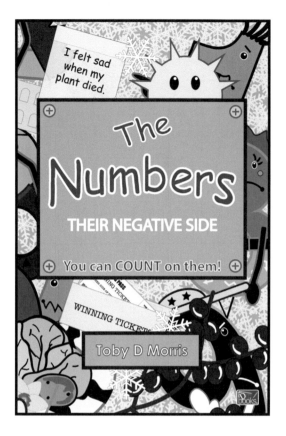

ISBN: 9781909286344

THE NUMBERS:
THEIR NEGATIVE SIDE!

The sun **rarely shines** on the **other side of the world**. So it's not surprising that, in this **fourth book** of the series, many of the numbers there feel so, well, **negative** about things! Luckily, help is at hand with both **The Numbers** and **The Fractions** getting together to help bring a little sunshine (building) to their lives. Through their combined efforts, the lives of **The Negatives** soon change and become, as you would expect with such great help, a lot more **positive.**

ISBN: 9781909286115

THE NUMBERS: THE ODD ONES!

Most of us can be a little **'odd'** at times, and – in this **fifth book** of the series – **The Numbers** decide to celebrate all their weird and wonderful **'odd'** **habits** and hobbies by organising **The Numbers Hill Carnival!** However, when the day arrives, it soon becomes clear that things couldn't be any **stranger**... the weather unexpectantly takes a turn for the worse, the sun suddenly vanishes from the sky, and the **Monster Bear** float escapes down the hill, scaring every little number in sight! Indeed, nothing could be **odder** – until an unexplained light is seen ripping across the sky!

ISBN: 9781909286122

THE NUMBERS:
THE FINAL COUNTDOWN!

In the **sixth** and **final book** of the series, bright lights continue to rip through the sky above the town that is home to many **numbers**, **fractions**, and **negatives**. But it is only when the orbiting satellite is hit, and all communication fails, that many numbers' worlds are changed. After a series of **mindfulness** events to help **reprogramme** their brains to live without their **addictive gadgets**, a new, greater problem emerges – a giant piece of space debris is on course to **hit Earth**! What will happen when the **final countdown** clock returns to zero? As the ground shakes and they all mindfully hold hands, something quite **unexpected** happens...

Toby was born in Cambridge, England, but spent most of his childhood growing up in a small village in Essex. As you can probably guess, he loves writing, as well as creating new worlds from his rather active imagination. He loves to look up and explore 'real' planets too, and to contemplate the mysteries of the universe around us! Oh, he also enjoys going to the gym, having a 'proper' coffee in the morning, and spending time with friends...!